MW01126933

Grains Of Sand
The Fall Of Neve Dekalim

by
Shifra Shomron

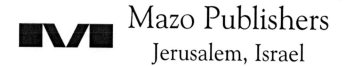

Mazo Publishers
Jerusalem, Israel

Grains Of Sand: The Fall Of Neve Dekalim
ISBN 978-965-7344-19-4
Text Copyright © 2007 - Shifra Shomron

Published by:
Mazo Publishers
Chaim Mazo, Publisher
P.O. Box 36084
Jerusalem 91360 Israel

Website: www.mazopublishers.com
Email: mazopublishers@gmail.com
Israel: 054-7294-565
USA: 1-815-301-3559

Contact The Author
Website: www.geocities.com/nevedekalim
Email: nevedekalim@yahoo.com

Cover Design by Frumi Chasidim
Background cover photograph by Or Yaakov Karni
Foreground cover photographs by Shifra Shomron

This book is dedicated to my family, friends, and neighbors who courageously lived in the Gush until the last grains of sand had slipped from our nation's shattered hourglass. And it is dedicated to all those who are loyally working to repair the hourglass pieces and scoop up some more sand.

About The Author

S hifra Shomron is an American-born writer who lived with her family in Neve Dekalim from 1992 until the tragic Disengagement in 2005. She loved her life in Gush Katif where she happily lived her childhood to her teenage years.

Shifra is a recipient of the *Letter of Academic Excellence* from the Ministry of Education in Israel. When *Grains Of Sand: The Fall Of Neve Dekalim* was first published, Shifra was enrolled in an accelerated college teaching program to become a high school English teacher in Israel.

Her previous literary works, articles, and poems have appeared in newspapers and websites. *Fronds in the Breeze* won first place runner-up in a youth contest.

Shifra is the second of seven children.

Table Of Contents

Regional Map
Of Southern Israel

Author's Preface

I started writing this book, *Grains Of Sand: The Fall Of Neve Dekalim*, in Nissan 5765 (April 2005) and finished it a year later in Nissan 5766 (April 2006). The tragic events regarding Gush Katif and their bitter aftermath burned in me, forcing me to take pen in hand and spill the burning lava of my thoughts and emotions onto white paper. As I wrote, my thoughts took form and shape; and the book became richer and the plot clearer.

This book is not about terror. In Gush Katif we lived in the shadow of terror for five years. We experienced stone throwing on the road, shooting on the road, Arab infiltrations, roadside bombs, knife stabbings, more than 5,000 mortars and kassam rockets... yet this book is not about terror. I do not mean to belittle neither the Arab attacks nor the pain of Jews wounded and/or killed, yet in writing a book about Gush Katif I do not focus on terror – because the people of the Gush did not let it affect their lives! It seems remarkable, incredible, even impossible, but it is true. Mortars fell as children walked to school, as children walked home and as children played outside with friends. Some people were injured – some were even killed by different forms of Arab attacks. But even the mortars did not fall every day and so we continued to go to school, to go to the beach, to go on walks and go about our daily errands about town. We did not ignore the terror – we *could not* ignore the terror, but we did not allow it to disrupt our lives.

This book is about a Gush Katif family. Much of the dialogue

The now destroyed Shomron family home in Neve Dekalim

is true. Most of the events are true to my family. The remaining events are true to others whose identities have been changed to protect their privacy. The portrayal of any characters in this book is not meant to resemble any living person. The closeness, the harmony, the sweetness of this family as well as the sorrow, the worries and the pain are true to life – true to my life.

I can only hope that my book be a faithful portrayal of the years before and during Disengagement. Many threads are woven into *Grains Of Sand: The Fall Of Neve Dekalim* – some are dark and some bright, some thick and some thin, some dull and some that sparkle. Dear reader, gaze carefully at my tapestry, stare with wonder and respect, touch gently and gingerly. Because it tells the tale of a vibrant community now smashed to gray piles of rubble. Because it tells the tale of people whose flowers were picked, whose saplings were hewn and, in the end, whose roots were cruelly ripped out.

Because Neve Dekalim has fallen.

Shifra Shomron
Nitzan Caravilla site
Sivan 5766
(June 2006)

Grains Of Sand
By Shifra Shomron

Grains and grains of golden sand
White foam of waves spraying
My roots are deep in you, my land,
Like the acacia near me swaying.

Few weeds: some here there more
Scattered by nature's careless hand
"A Scotland for the poor"
Yet I love you, my land.

A desert arid and bare
With a special grace and charm
My memories you share
Of times of joy and times of harm.

Tracks of turtle and of snake
Tracks of man, child and pet
See the pattern that they make
Don't destroy that pattern yet!

The people simple and sweet
Sometimes foolish, always kind.
You they'll always be glad to greet
The same fate does you bind.

Our lives so calmly passed here
Like the gentle waves of sea
Then, drowned in five years of fear
Outward calmness hid the torrent in me.

Red tiled roofs how snug you lie
Upon walls so very white!
Here we live and here some die
As to keep you we still fight.

Oh seashells pink and fair
Oh blossoms gold and round
When mortars fall who would dare
To lift you from the ground?

I hide inside my room
Until they say "all clear."
Or just ignore the boom
Though danger is quite near.

And fences all around me;
We are caged in like a lion.
They say it's for our safety
Can this be happening in Zion?!

I feel so alone;
Arab and Jew hate us.
We're to be tossed like a bone
With very little fuss.

Prayer vigils, blocking streets,
Orange streamers, going door to door
During sunshine and during sleets
How to save us? We aren't sure.

Still, a plover in the sky
Curiously looks down
The Gush seen from high
Is like a diamond in a crown!

Oh grains and grains of golden sand
What is to be my fate?
Shall I lose you from my land
Shall I lose you from my state?

Part I
Neve Dekalim:
The Best Kept Secret

Chapter 1

Yoram Yefet carefully opened the wooden gate, reached down and pet the adorable family dog Rufus and proceeded up the red brick walkway towards his house.

From the third bedroom the clear, rich sounds of a clarinet floated through the open window. A klezmer melody with plenty of lilts and twirls to it. Yoram smiled tiredly. He was glad that his wife Miri had convinced him into buying the kid a clarinet, even if he'd had to check an extra ten dunams of lettuce, making sure it was bug-free, to pay for it. Yair practiced regularly – about two hours a day. His music teacher at the community center was delighted with him. According to him, Yair had taken to the clarinet "like a fish to water." Trust Miri, Yoram thought wryly.

And with that thought in mind, Yoram carefully shook the hothouse dirt from his faded brown boots and entered the house.

He was a middle aged man of medium height with light brown hair and green eyes. He generally wore a solid colored short sleeved shirt, blue work pants and faded brown boots.

"Hi Yoram, dinner's almost ready," Miri called out to him from sorting the just-brought-in laundry in the living room.

"Good. I've brought some lettuce home. Whatever you can't use give to the turtles." And Yoram went back outside to water the garden.

That evening after dinner, Yoram and his daughter Efrat walked around the garden. The sun was setting – a huge round ball of gold sinking into the brilliant azure Mediterranean sea. The rest of the sky over the sea was splashed with crimson and royal purple, while further east the sky was growing dark and twinkling stars were slowly starting to appear. A soft wind was blowing off the sea shaking the naked branches of the tall trees and sending Efrat's long wavy brown hair into her brown almond shaped eyes. Impatiently she drew her hair back into a long ponytail and gazed up at the boughs of the tree they were standing under.

"See, *Aba*, there at the tip of the branch?"

"Where? Oh yes. I see. New buds, nice."

"The first signs of spring, *Aba*. We didn't see any on the other trees though."

"Well, you have to give them more time, Effie."

Efrat smiled to herself at the nickname her father had given her. It was her own special pet name. And as her father knew well, patience was *not* something that came naturally to her. She glanced at him suspiciously, but he had already moved on to the next tree, the last in the front yard.

Miri, drying her hands on a towel, came out to join them. She was a pretty woman, very petite, with an optimistic nature.

"Well, dear, why don't *you* go to Efrat's parent-teacher conference for a change?" Miri mischievously suggested to her husband.

"No thank you. That is your department. I work hard all day long and really can't find the time," Yoram answered hastily, slightly alarmed.

"*Ima*, I've told you already," Efrat moaned, "You don't honestly have to go. It'll only be a two minute meeting anyhow; long enough for my teacher to praise me and for you to feel uncomfortable and not sure as to what you ought to say! Don't bother, really."

"I know all that," Miri answered cheerfully, "But you know I feel I ought to go. And I am always glad to hear praises of my smart, beautiful Efrat-errific!" she ended smiling.

"What is all this about?" Yair asked, strolling nonchalantly over to meet them with a shining clarinet carefully held in one hand.

"Nothing," Efrat answered hastily. "Just talking about my parent-teacher conference which is coming up Tuesday."

"Oh! Sheesh! That reminds me. I've got one on Thursday at 6:00 p.m.," Yair said, digging a small crumpled piece of paper out of his pants pocket while he spoke. "*Aba* will you come? There's a short *shiur* beforehand...but the food will be good."

Efrat smiled to herself. It was so typical of Yair to add that about the food. As if *Aba* would go because of the food, she thought to herself, amused. But, she was now grinning, I bet it's the reason why Yair's going too…

"Of course he'll go," Miri said quickly, giving her husband a twinkling look. "I'll go to Efrat's and he'll go to yours."

Woof! Rufus barked loudly from inside the house. *Woof!* Beastie, the other house dog – a small, dark mutt – joined the chorus.

"Come on, Efrat," said Yair going back to the house. "Let's take Rufus and Beastie for a walk," Yair suggested to Efrat. "That way we can talk for a bit."

"Fine. Put your clarinet away properly first." And Efrat slowly redid her ponytail while waiting for Yair to put the dogs on their leashes.

The sun had sank behind the sea completely and all the stars were out in the dark spring sky, twinkling brightly. The cheerful shouts of kids playing echoed through the streets, and the sharp trilling of an unseen plover rang from the sky.

"Stop pulling, Rufus!" Efrat said while tugging Rufus closer to her. "Yair, why don't you let me have Beastie instead? He's moody and temperamental, but I always prefer taking *him* on a walk; *he* hardly pulls."

"Fine. No prob," Yair said absentmindedly. "But you're mis-taken if you think Rufus pulls," Yair said awakening. "He's nothing compared to Beauty! Did *Aba* tell you what happened when we took Beauty out for a walk yesterday?"

"No, he didn't. I was at the *Ulpana* until late yesterday."

"Well, it's sort of funny. We had her on her leash and she had a choke collar on too, but the minute *Aba* opened the gate to let her out, she just rushed forwards – pulling *Aba*. As soon as we were out in the sand dunes, *Aba* let her loose."

"Didn't the choke collar bother her at all?"

"No. She completely ignored it. You know, they say that golden retrievers are supposed to be highly trainable, intelligent dogs. Go figure!"

"You know, I think Beauty just puts on an act. She probably enjoys acting more foolish than she really is!"

"You know, Efrat, I think you are right. She actually is smart about certain things."

"Sure. She knows the words 'walk', 'food', 'treat' – everything that is important to her." Efrat laughed. "So, Yair, how are things at school? Will *Aba* be disappointed or delighted at your parent-teacher conference?"

"He's going to be bored to tears. My grades are good except for in *Gemara*; I got a 70 in my last test."

"Never mind. How are you in Hebrew grammar?"

Yair grinned broadly. "I got an 80! It was the eighth wonder of the world! Well," he said thoughtfully, changing the topic, "which way do we continue now?"

They had reached a point where they could continue straight, or they could leave the paved road and turn down a brick path.

"Whichever way our feet take us," Efrat mused slowly. "Tell you what, let's turn here," she said decidedly in a quick tone. "I love this long brick path. There are tall hedges on both sides, the houses are big and interesting and the lamps stuck in the middle of the dark thick hedges give the gardens an eerie look."

Yair silently agreed with her. The time to go down this path in the villa neighborhood was at night. Then you could really see the stars because the short electric street lights in the hedges didn't give off enough light to dull the light of the stars.

They walked silently for awhile enjoying the familiar sound of the slapping of their sandaled feet on the brick path, the dogs panting and the crickets chirping.

"Yair, "Efrat broke the silence. "Have you decided which *Yeshiva* you are going to attend next year?"

"I can't decide between going to the Katif Yeshiva here in the Gush or going away to the Lomed Yeshiva," Yair replied troubled.

"I think you should go away to the Lomed Yeshiva," Efrat said thoughtfully. "You'll be more independent and make new friends."

"Yes, well, I have to get accepted first," Yair said shortly.

"Remember when I was in sixth grade and you were in fourth grade and we used to walk to school together?" Efrat said tactfully changing the subject.

It was a rhetorical question. Neither of them would ever forget those early morning walks down the hill and to the school. They'd tell stories the entire way and watch the sun rise – fresh and brilliant. Few people were up and about – only a few early risers returning from the first *minyan*.

"Remember," Efrat continued, "How whenever we were in a hurry it took us more time to get to school. And whenever we tried our best to dawdle, we'd actually get there very quickly!"

"Sure I remember," Yair grinned. "We'd actually timed it once. It's a scientific fact that we discovered; the Efrat and Yair rule."

"And we'd be so busy talking on the way there that we wouldn't even notice passing by the synagogue and the town center and the *Mikva*!" Efrat smiled.

"And you always used to look in that puddle where the path turns sharply by the Yemenite synagogue," Yair accused her. "How come?"

Efrat smiled. "You wouldn't believe me."

"Try me!" Yair eagerly challenged his sister.

"Fine," she sighed. "It's actually pretty childish. I'd read in a book that there's a certain pond that if you looked in it you wouldn't see your own reflection; you'd see mountains and seven stars. So I'd, um…" she hesitated, purposely not looking at her brother's face.

"Try it out myself," Yair loudly finished for her.

"Precisely," Efrat agreed, still avoiding looking at her brother.

Yair started roaring with laughter. "See, Efrat, that's what happens when you read too much – it fries your brains!"

"Oh, shut up!" Efrat replied coolly, trying hard not to laugh also. Her brother's laughter was contagious and she generally couldn't help but join in. "As if you never did foolish things yourself," she retorted.

"Effie's trying not to smile…" Yair teased her. "I *see* you smiling," he added in a sing song.

"Well, I told you it was actually pretty childish," Efrat said, giving up and smiling. "But you needn't make such a fuss. It's embarrassing. Anyhow, what time is it?" She asked quickly, as Yair seemed about to start roaring with laughter again at her last comment.

"It's quarter to nine."

"Hmm. Better start heading home."

At the gate to the house Yair suddenly stopped. "Hey Effie, I've got a brilliant idea! Let's fill the bathtub with water and then we'll both look in it. You never know…"

Efrat gave him a sharp jab with her elbow and laughing the two of them cheerfully walked up the red brick walkway to the sleepy house.

Chapter 2

The next morning at breakfast, they were all busy eating scrambled eggs and toast when they were interrupted by a soft scratch at the front door. Efrat quickly got up to open the door and let Rufus into the house. Rufus came trotting cheerfully in, slightly wet from the morning dew on the lawn, and with twigs and leaves clinging to his soft fur because he had been sprawled out under the hedge, with his head poked out through the fence so as to see the people going by.

"Well, Yair," Yoram stopped eating and looked inquiringly at his son, "Which *Yeshiva* is it going to be next year?"

"I don't really know yet, *Aba*," Yair said shortly.

"Have you gotten a response from the Lomed Yeshiva yet?"

"No. But I've gotten accepted to the *Yeshiva* here in the Gush."

"So stay here in Gush Katif. I'd rather you stayed closer to home anyhow. Katif Yeshiva is only a seven minute drive from our home," Yoram advised cheerfully.

"Wait a second," Miri interrupted smoothly, while setting another platter of scrambled eggs on the table. "There are many advantages to staying in Gush Katif and there are also many advantages to going to the Lomed Yeshiva. However it is completely Yair's decision to make. *Aba* and I will be happy to point out advantages and disadvantages to both places, but in the end Yair has to make the choice. And *Aba* and I will be pleased with whatever choice you make."

"Uh, thanks, *Ima*."

Yoram got up and cleared his plate, putting it neatly in the bin. Efrat did likewise, and thoughtfully followed him outside.

"*Aba*, I don't think it's quite fair; Yair knows that you prefer him staying locally, and that Ima and I would rather he go away to the Lomed Yeshiva. It's not going to be easy for him to make up his mind," she said sadly.

Yoram listened without replying. She was right, he knew, but he felt obliged to try to prevent Yair from making a decision that he would, perhaps, later regret.

"What time do you come home from the *Ulpana* today, Effie?" Yoram asked her out loud.

"Around 3:00, why?"

"Then we'll take Beauty out this afternoon."

"Lovely! She got upset last night when Yair and I took Rufus and Beastie out, and she was left behind," Efrat said, delighted. "How is my mint doing?"

"It is growing well. I gave it fertilizer yesterday. If you don't want the flowers, cut them off. You'll get more leaves that way."

"Well, I want the leaves for mint tea, so I suppose I'll take the flowers off," she said thoughtfully. "But if I forget, do it for me please."

"Fine." And Yoram put his backpack into his green bike basket and wheeled off to check the lettuce in a couple hothouses in the nearby community of B'dolach.

Efrat went over to her next door neighbor's house. She only had about fifteen minutes in which to water the garden before going to the *Ulpana*. Since last night she had seen buds on a shade tree, she wanted to make sure that if her neighbor's garden didn't grow it would not be from lack of water. She watered quickly and hurried down to the *Ulpana*.

That afternoon was very eventful with Beauty in the sand dunes. It was hot out and Yoram's, Efrat's and Yair's faces were soon flushed and sweat trickled in streams from their foreheads. Efrat's brown eyes keenly studied the golden sand lying before her sandaled feet. Yoram readjusted his straw hat and Yair wiped his sweaty face with the sleeve of his faded green T-shirt. They all continued searching; for the past twenty minutes they had been carefully studying the varied tracks that the different animals had left behind them. They were looking for a reptile – a creature that they could eagerly take home and add to the reptiles already in their outdoor terrarium.

Yoram carefully stepped over a low bush in his way. Yair, not avoiding the bush quite so neatly, followed. Efrat followed their lead, but suddenly stopped, her right foot arrested in midair. Bending down she swiftly picked something up. Cupping it in the palms of her hands, she rushed up to her father and to her brother. Yoram and Yair were delighted, for in the palms of Efrat's small cupped hands lay a very tiny baby turtle! Yair gingerly touched it. Its shell was rough; not shiny and smooth like an adult turtle. It's color was dark green. It was tiny. And extremely cute. Amazing that I stepped right over it without seeing it, Yair mused to himself.

"Good eyes, Effie," Yoram complimented her.

"Thanks, *Aba*. Isn't he adorable!" Efrat smiled, delighted with her find.

Beauty, jealous of the attention being given to a creature other than herself, rushed over and tried to stick her substantial nose into Efrat's cupped hands. But Efrat raised her hands higher and Yoram sternly told Beauty, "No." For the rest of the walk in the dunes, Beauty stayed away from them and they had to coax her with a treat in order to put her back on her leash and return home.

Back at home, they gently placed the small turtle in their outdoor terrarium. They already had several fascinating chameleons and five large turtles in there. This was Yoram's special hobby. He delighted in rearranging it; adding smooth white pebbles to make a stream, moving the plants in different arrangements, leveling a valley, adding small hills…It was a small kingdom of which Yoram was the designer. His kids were extremely fond of it and took a lively interest in everything that went on in there. They fed the chameleons grasshoppers they caught in the sand dunes, and they fed the turtles vegetables that Yoram brought home from what was thrown away near the B'dolach hothouses he checked.

That evening after dinner, Yair disappeared from the house and Efrat went into her room to study for a history test. She sat down on the comfortable dark blue chair. Opening her backpack, she took out a thick black book with the golden title *The Second Temple Period and Rebellion* emblazoned on it. She also took out her light blue, two ringed folder in which were her neat, critiqued notes of everything her history teacher had taught them in the past six months. Several girls in her class had xeroxed her notes in order to study for the test. Her classmates just didn't find neither the material nor the teacher to be interesting. In fact, while the teacher droned on about Horcenus and Aristoblus, the classroom sank into a drowsy stupor – all except for Efrat, who sat in the front row listening with rapt attention, critiquing the material with precision, and occasionally asking a question which caused the teacher to beam at her and to launch into a long monotonous explanation.

Efrat opened her history book to page 93 and started reading out loud to herself. When she finished reading the chapter, she turned to her notes and read them out loud also. Satisfied, she proceeded to the next chapter. Slowly, the peaceful surroundings of her small pretty bedroom faded. In her mind's eye, Efrat saw Pompeius leading vast numbers of Roman legions to Jerusalem. She saw their glinting spears, their bright shields and heard the steady tramp, tramp of their feet. She saw the frightened faces of the Jewish defenders, determined to protect their Holy city and their independence. She saw them clashing with their fellow Jewish brothers preventing them from opening the gates of the city to the Roman legions. The people behind the city walls were divided! There wasn't a unified front against the Romans! The city hadn't a chance...

Suddenly Efrat's bedroom door banged open and Yair came in.

"Oh!" Efrat jumped. "I didn't know you had come home. Where were you?"

"I went to check our mail," Yair answered soberly.

"Did we get anything interesting?"

"Yes, I got a letter from the Lomed Yeshiva. In order to get in I would have to retest in *Gemara*."

"That is crazy!" Efrat cried out appalled.

"I think so. I've made up my mind; I'm going to the Katif

Rufus

Yeshiva."

Efrat smiled gently. "Well," she said, "at least we'll be close enough to see each other often. Have you told *Aba*? He'll be delighted!"

"Yes, I've told *Ima* and *Aba*. And, Effie," Yair said grinning

Beastie

widely, "you have no idea what a relief it is to have this settled at last!"

Efrat nodded a trifle impatiently. "Yair, I am really delighted for you, but, please, I have an important history test..."

So Yair went out to call several classmates and spread the news. He then went outside to romp with Beauty and Efrat returned to studying the second Temple period and rebellion.

Beauty

Chapter 3

Spring sped by swiftly that year. The trees finished carefully adorning themselves in their pleasant garments of blossoms and leaves, the weeds multiplied and covered the golden face of the sand dunes, leaving Efrat wondering at this quick transformation from aridity to fertility, and the bright sun and cloudless blue skies graced many swiftly passing spring days.

Efrat finished her history, math and Bible tests with distinction, Yair did well in everything but slightly less well in *Gemara* and Hebrew grammar. Yoram continued checking lettuce, cabbage, celery and green-onion, and Miri and her friend Mrs. Eisley took to meeting several times a week to exercise together in order to lose the winter fat they'd put on.

In fact, Miri and Mrs. Eisley weren't the only ones in Gush Katif that were bent on exercise that spring; every night the Yefet family would see many women and several couples taking brisk walks up the hill and past the Yefet family house. These walks were an excellent opportunity for Gush Katifnics to socialize as well as to try and lose a few kilograms.

It always amused Efrat and Yair to see how many people preferred the talking over the walking – as you could clearly see by their slower pace and brisker chatter. Both Efrat and Yair honestly believed that the best way to get into shape was to go running or jogging. Several times a week, the kids and Yoram would take Beauty out to the lonely white gravel road at the edge of the sand dunes. They would let Beauty loose and try and keep up with her as they jogged up and down the slopes of the white gravel road; their sneakers going swiftly down the slopes and toiling slowly up the slopes. They didn't chatter as they jogged; they saved the talking for the walk home as they returned by the same route.

Swiftly, too swiftly perhaps, spring drew to a graceful close and summer arrived. No more exercising, treks in sand dunes or concentrating on schoolwork; the days were hot, the sun beat down mercilessly, and it didn't cool down very much in the night either. Yair had to stop walking around barefoot – the grains of sand imitated the sun with their color and their temperature too successfully – and bought himself a pair of handsome leather sandals.

The Yefet family took their three dogs out on walks only in the early morning or in the late evening. The dogs passed most of the hot summer days sprawled out on the cool tiled floor in the Yefet family house, occasionally getting up to lap some water from their silver colored metal water dishes which were constantly kept full.

One day, Efrat and Yair came happily home with their report cards. The school year was over! Yoram and Miri read the report cards, beamed, signed them and stored them in the family files. Efrat and Yair celebrated the end of the school year over pizza, ice cream and cola. Several plovers gliding over the house trilled louder than usual; summer vacation had arrived!

The next day after rising a bit later than usual and *davening* and breakfasting a bit later than usual too, Efrat and Yair got some paper and a pencil and sat down together at Efrat's desk.

Efrat wrote in big bold letters across the top of the page: **Plans for the Summer Vacation** and underlined it twice.

"Well," she said looking up from the page and turning to Yair. "Any ideas?"

"Sure!" he replied eagerly. "Let's build our last fort this summer. I know we've already built about a million of them over the years, but they were all rather childish. Now we are old enough and have enough experience to build a *really* good one!"

"Excellent idea," Efrat said slowly and approvingly. "But we have to decide where to build it and out of which materials. You are going into ninth grade and I'm going into eleventh. This will probably be the last time we build a fort and it has to be our best one ever."

"Oh, I agree," Yair replied emphatically. "But choosing the location and materials are the fun part of building a fort! I think building in an acacia tree would be the best. Tomorrow we'll start looking for a likely one."

#1 Build a fort. Efrat wrote down. "O.K. what else?"

"Well," Yair replied, "we should have a decent schedule. You know, have a sports hour and a homework hour – for all the horrid assignments the teachers gave us, and a movie hour and a lunch hour…" he trailed off.

"We try that every year and we never stick to it," Efrat said, grinning ruefully.

"Well, we shall this time," Yair said determinedly. "But include blank hours too, for us to do what we wish in them. Perhaps that will help us."

"Fine. I'll work on it this evening," Efrat replied, putting the pencil away and leaving the paper on her desk.

They got up and went to the living room.

"It is too hot," Efrat sighed. "I haven't the energy to do anything."

"Why don't we all go to the beach?" Miri called from the kitchen where she was washing the breakfast dishes. "I'll call Mrs. Eisley and see if she'll drive us there."

Yoram and Miri Yefet refused to own a car, claiming that it was very expensive, that they wouldn't walk a meter if they owned one, and that they could get by without it. Therefore Yoram bicycled to go check certain B'dolach hothouses every morning (about a fifteen minute bike ride), Efrat and Yair walked to their schools and if anyone of the Yefet family left the Gush it was usually by bus or by hitchhiking.

Happily, Mrs. Eisley was only too delighted to drive them to the beach. She had been cleaning the house for several guests she expected over, and the thought of a few hours of relaxation at the beach with Miri Yefet sounded most enjoyable.

Gazing out the car windows as they sped past sand, hot houses and palm trees, Efrat sighed. "It is not fair," she said hotly, anger flashing in her big brown eyes. "This is our land. Ours! G-d promised it to every single one of our forefathers! And after two thousand years of exile, we finally return to our land and establish a state, and yet in Gush Katif Jews cannot walk the fifteen minute walk from our community of Neve Dekalim to the sea. It makes me furious."

"I know," Yair said quietly. "Some kids from the nearby settlements of Netzer Hazani, Katif and Ganei Tal do walk from their homes to the beach – because they only have a five minute walk and they do it as a group. But we," he continued bitterly, "the few times a year that the people of Neve Dekalim walk to the sea we have an army escort the entire way!"

"I really dislike it!" Efrat whispered. "The Arabs all gather in front of their houses smirking, their eyes glittering with malice, just sitting there and watching us Jews walk by. And we – with our soldiers on every rooftop, by every building, escorted on all sides we walk down to the sea. 'A free people in our land' humph!"

"I don't like it either," Yair replied steadily. "Perhaps one day it will change."

"Not until our government officials return to their roots and learn to be proud G-d-fearing Jews," Efrat said sadly, "And heaven only knows when that will happen because – I – don't!"

"Here we are!" Miri trilled out happily. "Just feel the breeze!"

Efrat and Yair rushed out of the car and raced to the entrance. Here they separated; Yair going left to the mens' beach and Efrat turning right to the women's beach. The separate gender beaches allowed religious Jews to bathe in modesty according to Jewish Law. Miri and Mrs. Eisley followed cheerfully a bit more slowly behind.

The blue waves glistened invitingly and smashed onto the wet sand. The hot sun rays caressed several girls lying on towels interested in tanning themselves yet a darker shade. A number of younger girls squealed happily as they jumped in the waves, and further out in the sea, a few women were swimming diligently. At the end of the horizon, the deep blue of the sea met the light blue of the sky. There wasn't a cloud in the sky, and several gulls soared overhead. Grinning, Efrat changed to her swim clothes and ran recklessly down the beach to the sea. Flopping herself down on the wet sand within reach of the waves, Efrat leaned back onto her elbows and stared out over the sea. Pulling her ponytail holder out of her hair, she let the refreshingly cool sea breeze ripple through her long wavy brown hair. Squinting, Efrat saw that there was one girl who was rather far out.

"Hey! You in the green shirt, come back!" the life guard bellowed. TWEET, he blew his whistle, "Come on back!"

"Hello!" Miri cheerfully plopped down by her daughter. "Wow! Look at this wave coming at us, it's huge!"

So it was, this new wave gathering power and speed as it rushed to the shore. As it enveloped the smaller waves around it, it rose up until...*smash* the wave broke and, reaching Efrat and Miri, lifted them gently off the sand. As the wave receded, it turned them around a bit.

Efrat and Miri laughed. "Well, sweetie, I'm going off to try and swim for a bit," Miri said. "When you get hungry, lunch is in my backpack under a frond beach shade. Yair has his lunch in his backpack."

Efrat nodded. "Thanks, have fun."

Efrat was quiet on the way home. Yair chatted about the jelly-fish he had seen, the fish his friend had caught and the pranks some kids had played on the life guard. Surprised at Efrat's silence, Yair looked at her. She was staring out the car window at the sprawling Arab encampment.

Chapter 4

Next morning Yair returned home from the synagogue to find Efrat finishing her breakfast.

"O.K," she said briskly when she saw him. "I've put the schedule on the refrigerator."

Yair gazed at the fridge. On a big white piece of paper was a neat red grid. Inside each box was Efrat's neat round handwriting in thin black marker. He looked closer.

"Efrat!" He complained, "What are all these library hours?"

Efrat looked at him, surprised. "Well, really, Yair, it's what I generally do in my free time. You know that."

Yair grinned. "Efrat, you're the weirdest person I know. Who else would voluntarily spend time in the library during summer vacation?!"

Efrat ignored her brother, and took another bite of her toast.

And so it was that while Yair spent most of the cooler morning and evening hours building a wooden fort around the dark brown branches of a sturdy acacia tree, Efrat spent hour after hour in the studious section of the small local library, deeply engrossed in the history of the two anti-British underground groups in pre-state Israel.

"This is fascinating!" Efrat whispered to herself, deeply engrossed in the history of the National Military Organization and the Freedom Fighters of Israel. "These people were amazing!" she said with feeling, grinning with admiration, pride and amusement as she read of Dov, "the tall blonde," rescuing Dr. Israel Eldad, the ideological leader of the Freedom Fighters of Israel.

Eldad had been arrested by the British while he was in a high school still working as a teacher. Trying to escape, he ran to a nearby student's house and, as the British approached, he flung open the three story high window and attempted descending by sliding down the drainpipe. He lost his grip and fell! Miraculously still alive, he was taken to Hadassah Hospital where the doctors had to fit a cast onto his back. The British would escort him from the Latrun jail to a medical checkup in Jerusalem every several months. The freedom fighters used this knowledge in their plans to rescue him. With Dov as commander, two men wearing white robes entered the clinic while carrying a "wounded" man on a stretcher. Suddenly cured, the "wounded" man leapt off the stretcher and drew a pistol, as did the two men escorting him. They quickly overpowered the policemen at the door and the sergeant sitting by Eldad. The women in the waiting room started screaming. Eldad ran to the door. He was in the yard. He ran. Several men who were waiting for him outside, surrounded him and showed him the way. A car was waiting. He jumped in. The handcuffs still dangled from his left hand. The car was crammed with the men and with the guns taken from the overpowered guards. Someone shouted to the driver to step on it. The driver did. That same someone fell on Eldad's neck and called out that he was now even with Eldad. It was Dov! Before Eldad could figure out why Dov was "even" with him, Dov commanded them to be silent and bend down. A bullet went through the roof of the car. But the car had already done several turns and was in the quiet, empty alleyways. The car stopped. Dov and Eldad switched to a second, waiting car. Again the driver was commanded to step on it, and after several minutes, they were out of the city.

"Fantastic fellows," Efrat mused to herself. "Such devotion! They risked everything – a nice quiet life, a successful career, a peaceful family life, freedom, their very lives – all so that the vision of a Jewish state in Israel would cease to be a vision, and instead be a live and beautiful reality. And what did happen in their future?" She smiled rather sadly. Dov was killed in the War of Independence as a commander in the IDF down in the Negev, away from his bleeding and beloved Jerusalem. And Eldad? Ben Gurion had tried to prevent him from resuming his pre-state employment as a teacher since, though an extremely talented teacher, he was not "one of theirs," but rather a right wing extremist… This was typical. Many ex-underground members lost their lives in the War of Independence in which 1% of Israel's' Jewish population was killed. Others found it extremely difficult to find a job as the ruling socialist party hated and hounded them.

Efrat sighed. It upset her; these precious young, dedicated fellows who almost alone bore the heavy burden of bringing a state into being, amazingly succeeded in doing so, and yet remained almost as unknown and unthanked as when they had been unknown soldiers in the underground.

"Still," Efrat nodded determinedly, "not unknown to me! Or unthanked; I shall mark the days of their passing away whether they were shot by British bullet, hanged by British rope or killed by Arabs. For every one of them that fell was another step that advanced us towards our destination of freedom in our resurrected state!"

And nodding her head silently once more, Efrat eagerly resumed reading on the rescue of Dr. Israel Eldad.

For years after, Efrat would find strength and courage in remembering the long struggle of the NMO and FFI for Israel's independence. In these unknown soldiers she found an undying source of potent, authentic Jewish pride. For who could fail to be moved by reading that the last three Jews to be hanged (last because the NMO finally hanged two British soldiers in retaliation) by the British: Avshalom Haviv, Meir Nakar and Ya'acov Weis shouted to their fellow cellmates in Acre prison: "Be strong! We won't shame!" several hours before they were hanged.

High up in the clear blue sky a spur winged plover trilled sharply and musically. Swooping lower, it glided swiftly way out to the golden sand dunes.

Since it was summer, the only green to be seen in the dunes was the dark green of the long and slender acacia leaves drooping slightly under the sun's long and steady gaze. Glinting whitely between the grains of sand were many fragments of seashells, remnants of the time when these glowing sand dunes had been a cool ocean bed. Of that once mighty sea only the seashells remained as a last witness amidst the long swaying acacia branches and crumbling brown logs. At nights when all was still, perhaps the not-so-distant sounds of the breaking waves reminded the sea shell fragments of their forgotten past under the rolling gray waves. Perhaps they were gently lulled to sleep on the soft pale sand under the twinkling stars with the roaring of the sea a soothing and familiar lullaby in the background. And perhaps they dreamed of the day when the sea would once more retake the land it had lost.

Chapter 5

That summer Yair finished his fort, his last tribute to a merry childhood. The fort met with Efrat's approval and they would go there together with a picnic lunch and a game or book. Efrat loved climbing up the ladder nailed to the trunk of the tree and clambering onto the sturdy branch. Sitting there she could look out over the whole sand dunes, see the sea, feel the clean fresh sea breeze, see the red roofs of houses in the section of Neve Dekalim by the *Ulpana* and a comforting feeling of peace would engulf her.

The hot summer months passed and the month of Elul (September) arrived. Elul, the month of *Tshuva*, of fixing one's wrong behavior. The month of which it is said that "the King is in the Field" – that the Lord of Hosts is near to all and that it is easy to be forgiven. The last month before the Day of Judgment. The Sephardi men got up early while it was still dark out to blow the shofar and recite *Slichot*. The Ashkenazi men had three more weeks before they did so too. The housewives were busy with the meal preparations for all the holidays of the upcoming month of Tishrei. The children learned how the first month of the Jewish New Year is a special day; not celebrated by partying and by getting drunk, but rather by holiness – by asking for forgiveness and for a good new year, by eating symbolic food, by *davening* special prayers, by blowing the shofar and by doing *Tashlich*.

Indeed, the first day of the New Year is also the last day of the previous year and there must be a reckoning before one can proceed. And G-d does the reckoning of every man and woman, but in His mercy gives a grace period of ten days until Yom Kippur, the Day of Atonement, on which He seals the verdict drawn up on Rosh Hashanah, the New Year.

The Yefet family cleaned their house and asked forgiveness from each other and from all their friends. Yair returned home from Katif Yeshiva in time to help Miri and Efrat with the cooking.

"Now, put on a big pajama shirt before you *touch* those pomegranates," Miri insisted. "They stain!"

"Okay," Yair grumbled.

Efrat and Yair each sat down with a cutting board, a sharp
knife, a large bowl and several round red pomegranates.

Efrat sliced one open and then cut it into smaller sections.

"Gorgeous!" She exclaimed, looking down at the ruby red
seeds. Deftly she started separating the seeds into the large bowl.
Yair carefully cut one open too.

"You know," Efrat grinned, "I've heard that there are 613 seeds
in a pomegranate – equal to the commandments in the Torah.
Would you like to count?"

"Are you kidding?" Yair looked up, aghast. "Anyhow, the sym-
bolism of the pomegranate is: May our merits increase like a pomegranate."

"True," Efrat agreed, picking a white piece of pomegranate out
from the bowl. "Do you know what time *Tashlich* is?"

"I'm not sure. You'll have to ask *Aba*."

"Would you two hurry up, please," Miri grimaced at them both.
"I still have the fish head and the apples and honey to prepare."

"Fish," Yair recited, "that we may be like the head and not the
tail."

"Apples and honey," Efrat recited quickly, not to be outdone
by her brother, "that we may have a sweet New Year."

And after finishing help prepare the symbolic food, Efrat quickly
went to water at her neighbor's blossoming garden, shower and dress
for the holiday.

*"I will not turn to destroy Ephraim: for I am G-d and not
man; the Holy One in the midst of thee: and I will not come as an
enemy." [Hoshea 11: 9]*

Part II
Second Intifada:
Life Goes On

Chapter 6

Several days later, Yair had returned to Katif Yeshiva. Efrat was a bit lonely as she stood outside the house at night and gazed up into the dark sky. A cool early autumn breeze blew, shaking the brown leaves on the grapevines and sending several floating to the sand beneath. Efrat shivered a bit. Her brown eyes, searching the night sky, suddenly fastened upon the crescent moon. Efrat stared, wide eyed: there was a most distinct red haze around the young moon, causing the moon to look as though it was dipped in blood. Efrat shivered again, but this time it had nothing to do with the wind.

A few weeks passed, and Yair returned home for Succot vacation. It was a grey windy day and Yair struggled to hold the wooden board Yoram was hammering.

"Let go a second," Yoram told Yair.

Silently they watched as the wind shook the *Succah*.

"Hmm, I think a few more nails would be a good idea," Yoram said, his green eyes appraising the *Succah* carefully.

"I think so too," Efrat grinned, handing him some more nails. "I don't want it to come crashing down on us!"

Yair chuckled. "Efrat, you think this is bad? You should see the dorms at our *Yeshiva*; the interior walls are plaster, so if you kick them, there's a large hole. In short, the Swiss cheese effect!"

Efrat laughed. "Boys!" She said cheerfully.

"No, no. Men!" Yair corrected, grinning and standing as tall as his almost fifteen years allowed him. "We are all past *Bar Mitzvah* at *Yeshiva*!"

"Try acting like it," Efrat retorted, her brown eyes twinkling merrily.

"There!" Yoram announced suddenly. "Now let the wind blow!"

During the week of Succot, Rotem Uchana and her brother Natanel walked over to the Yefets to visit with Efrat and Yair. Entering the gaily decorated wooden *Succah*, the four teenagers suddenly froze: they heard loud cracklings in the distance.

"What was that?!" Rotem asked nervously.

"Sounded like popcorn popping," Yair joked, trying to lighten the mood.

"Quiet!" Efrat commanded as the noise started again.

Mr. Yefet suddenly came bursting into the *Succah*. "Guys, that was gunshots you just heard!"

"Ours or theirs?" Efrat asked nervously.

"Probably both. Listen carefully and you'll hear two types of gunshot; one is probably the Arabs shooting and the other is presumably our soldiers," Yoram explained calmly.

"Mr. Yefet, can the bullets reach us?" Natanel asked, asking the question that was foremost in all their minds. They all watched Yoram anxiously, jumping as some more gunshots erupted.

Yoram considered thoughtfully. "No, I don't think so," he said at last. "Highly unlikely. And if a bullet did reach, I doubt it would have enough force to do more than maybe bruise."

"That's a relief!" Efrat smiled, looking a bit excited now instead of looking scared.

Miri suddenly joined them in the *Succah*.

"Rotem, Natanel, I'd like you two to please call your parents and tell them that you are safely at our house and won't leave until the shooting stops," Miri requested calmly.

"Sure, Mrs. Yefet," Rotem replied quickly and followed Miri into the house to telephone home.

"That was exciting," Yair commented to Efrat that evening after their guests had finally gone home.

"I wonder what it was all about," Efrat said quietly. "Do you think that there will be shooting again tomorrow?" She asked.

"Nah, I doubt it," Yair answered, almost regretfully. "I'm sure our soldiers have it under control by now."

But Yair was wrong. It was the start of a fresh New Year and the Arabs had once again declared war on the State of Israel. Not content with being defeated by the Jewish state in 1948, 1956, 1967,

1973 and in the first *Intifada*, the Arab population had now launched a second *Intifada* in the hopes of destroying the Jewish state.

Efrat and Yair and all the other children, youth, and adults in Gush Katif were to become very used to hearing gunshots, and quite expert in distinguishing between "ours" and "theirs."

On the 22nd of Cheshvan (November 20th), Efrat went to the *Ulpana* a bit nervous. She hadn't done very well on her last geography test (a 72), so her kind teacher Miriam had given her and several other classmates a chance to improve their grade by doing an activity for the class that was related to what they were learning. Efrat, Rachel and Reut had prepared a bingo and several other activities in their free time, and today was the day they were supposed to present it to the class.

However, amazingly, teacher Miriam didn't arrive on time for class. Efrat and Rachel looked for her throughout the *Ulpana* but didn't find her. Two girls from Efrat's grade came out of the restroom, sobbing hysterically and clutching their cell phones. They sobbingly admitted that they'd heard a rumor as to where teacher Miriam was, but they refused to tell, in case it wasn't true.

In the meantime, rumors spread quickly through the *Ulpana* hallways: "The K'far Darom school bus was attacked this morning... several people are dead...some are badly injured..."

Efrat's grade slowly gathered into their classroom and started saying Psalms. Many girls, fearing that the worst had happened to their beloved teacher, were sobbing at their desks.

Efrat didn't cry. She sat stiffly at her desk.

A bit later, the *Ulpana* principal entered their classroom. His face was grave. Slowly he told them that both Miriam and another teacher had been killed that morning when the Arabs set up a roadside bomb and fired upon the K'far Darom school bus. Several children were injured badly. School was over for the day, but the parents had to come to take their daughters home.

After the principal left the classroom, Efrat, Reut, and Rachel exchanged glances. Slowly, Rachel took out the bingo game, and the other activities that they had made and had intended to pass out to the class. Rachel walked over to the garbage can, tore up the papers and threw them in.

Efrat felt a strange empty feeling inside. She walked out of the class and over to the public phone.

"Hello, *Ima?*" she asked in a voice that sounded very calm and quite unlike her voice. "My teacher, Miriam, has been killed. The *Ulpana* is requiring parents to pick up their daughters. I need you and *Aba* to come to the *Ulpana* so I can go home," and she hung up. Shakily, she walked outside the building and waited in the cold sunshine by the green gates for her parents to come.

Efrat hadn't been able to cry in the classroom, but the minute she saw her mother's tear-stained face and felt the furious anger radiating from her father, she threw herself into her mother's arms.

"She was a great teacher, *Ima*, a really great teacher," she sobbed on the way home.

That night, the IAF and Navy hit targets in the Gaza Strip. The Arabs merely lost electricity and a few vacated buildings. Several Gush Katif residents, furious at the lack of a proper army response, ignited several Arab-owned hothouses. A couple of those men who had taken the law into their own hands were arrested.

Efrat writes in her diary
Motzei Shabbat, 27 Cheshvan (November 25)

Dear Memory,
This Shabbat, the parsha of Chayei Sarah, we had to stay in our houses all day; Arabs blew up an army outpost and shot at our houses. The IDF responded with tank fire, helicopters and rockets, but they shot anti-tank missiles and one of our officers was killed. Several from their side were killed. The noise that went on all day was incredible!

Sunday, 5 Tevet (December 31)

Dear Memory,
This is so horrid! A Rav, his wife and family were driving in their van in the Shomron hills when they were ambushed. Arabs shot at their vehicle – fifty bullets! The Rav was killed at once, the car fell into a ravine and turned over five times before it stopped! The wife was shot in the stomach and died. I think the children are all right, if one can call kids whose parents were murdered "all

right." They are so young and now they are orphans. Hashem, help them!

Monday, 20 Tevet (January 15)

Dear Memory,
Two Arabs tried to infiltrate Neve Dekalim through the gate. Very scary! They were both shot dead.
The Arabs hanged two Arabs that they accused of "friendly relations" with Israel. When asked why they were hanged, they replied: "Because it is a time of war." See, Mem, they declare it to be a time of war, and yet we don't!

Wednesday, 4 Nissan (March 26)

In Hevron, an infant was killed while in her father's arms. He was wounded badly in both legs. The family refuses to bury her until the army responds adequately. Oh, Mem, it is so shocking. The poor family! And such cruelty – an Arab sniper killing a Jewish baby. We haven't seen such hatred since World War Two – and yet now, unlike our situation in the Holocaust, we actually have the means to protect ourselves; thank Hashem, we have the strongest army in the Middle East. But we are so stupid!
Passover vacation starts today and Yair will be back from Yeshiva. I've missed him!
The garden is getting green again; spring!
My allergies are acting up because the olive trees are flowering...uncomfortable, but it'll pass soon enough.

~ ~ ~

That night, the fourth of Nissan (March 26), Yoram, Efrat, and Yair rushed outside their house at the sound of helicopters.
"Does anyone see them?" Efrat asked, searching the night sky.
"No," Yoram and Yair both answered.
"So this is the response for the murder of an innocent baby – helicopters flying around in circles?" Yair asked sarcastically.
"Wait a bit," Yoram advised. "Patience."

Yair opened his mouth to retort, but shut it as they all suddenly saw a bright light streaking down swiftly in the dark sky descending in the direction of K'han Yunis.

"1...2...3..."

Boom!!!!!!!!

The ground shook and a bright light rose up momentarily from K'han Yunis. Then the light faded and Yoram, Yair and Efrat exchanged excited glances.

"Excellent! Show those Arabs that Jewish blood is not cheap!" Yoram cried, as his green eyes flashed. "Killing children, babies..." he muttered to himself, "that is the lowest of the low."

"Look!" Efrat cried out, pointing up in the night sky. "See those sparks?"

"Those are so that any heat-seeking missiles that the Arabs fire will be attracted to those sparks and not to the army helicopters," Yoram explained.

"Ah," Efrat and Yair nodded their heads wisely.

By now everyone in the neighborhood had rushed out of their houses. Everyone stood, gazing up in the night sky in the direction from which they could hear the rumble of the army helicopters. They were all waiting for more missiles to be fired at Arab K'han Yunis. And sure enough, several more bright lights shot through the darkness. Everyone gazed, entranced. That is, they were entranced until the news the next morning when they heard that the army had warned the Arabs ahead of time which buildings were going to be bombed. Thus, no Arabs suffered loss of life.

"What a waste of bombs and helicopter fuel," Miri sighed.

"What is the matter with our leadership?" Yoram wondered. "Our children are being sniped and killed, and we retaliate by bombing empty buildings?"

"And I raised up of your sons for prophets, and of your young men for Nezirim. Is it not even thus, O you children of Israel? says the Lord. But you gave the Nezirim wine to drink; and commanded the prophets, saying, prophecy not." [Amos 2: 11-12]

Chapter 7

"Efrat, wake up please, you'll be late for school," Miri said as she opened the blinds in Efrat's room and let the fresh sun light stream in.

"What time is it?" Yair groaned sleepily from his room.

"It is 7:15," Miri replied. "What time do you need to get up, Yair?"

"Wake me up at 8:15. I'll catch the 8:30 *minyan*. Then I'll hitch hike to *Yeshiva* – I don't need to be there until 11:00."

Efrat slowly dressed, made her bed and organized her backpack. What a shame Passover vacation is over, she thought while brushing her long wavy brown hair. It passed so quickly – from one Arab attack to another – and a complete lack of adequate army response. She finished fastening her hair clip and hurried to the kitchen for breakfast.

"Effie, the weather is getting warmer, you'll want to water more often," Yoram advised his daughter.

Efrat nodded. "I'll go water right after I eat."

So after breakfast, Efrat walked down the red brick sidewalk, opened the wooden gate, closed it behind her and crossed the street to her neighbor's house. She opened her neighbor's rusty iron gate and walked up the red brick sidewalk. Then she picked up the long green hose and turned the water on full force. First she watered the mint growing in a large pot, next she watered the grapevine – its light green leaves just opening after the winter months. After that came the beautiful, tall, sturdy sunflowers that were turning their golden crowned heads towards the sun, then the jasmine and the citrus trees, and the fast spreading honeysuckle whose flower buds would open soon, and the desert adapted gerber, and the fig trees, and the two olive trees and so on.

"Finished!" she declared fifteen minutes later. And she returned to her house, gathered her backpack and her history folder, called out "Good-bye everyone" and as Yoram, Miri and Yair called out "Good-bye, have a good day" back at her, she hurried out the wooden gate and down the hill to the *Ulpana*. She passed the Eisley's pretty house – Mr. Eisley was leaving for the synagogue and Mrs. Eisley was playing the piano. She passed the big playground at the bottom of the hill – it was empty now. All Passover vacation it had been full of kids running and playing there shrieking cheerfully to each other. Now it was empty since school was resuming today. Efrat continued; past the playground and through the villa neighborhood.

"Hey, Efrat, wait up!" She heard a classmate of hers, Rachel, call out to her. Efrat waited for Rachel to catch up.

"How was your vacation?" Efrat asked Rachel.

"Great! We stayed at a hotel in Jerusalem for the first three days and then we visited relatives all over – in Beit Shemesh, Tsfat, Eli…"

"Sounds like fun."

"Oh, it was! How was your vacation? Did you go anywhere?"

"No, we stayed home. The vacation was O.K. but it seemed to pass so very quickly!"

"I know! I could have used another week of vacation at least!"

Efrat smiled but didn't reply. In a way she was glad Passover vacation was over. Too many Jews had gotten hurt by Arabs. It had completely ruined her Passover vacation.

Rachel pushed open the *Ulpana's* tall green gate, and they both smiled hello at the guard who was sitting in his booth by the gate, listening to music.

In their classroom was a cheerful buzz of many girls happily telling about their Passover vacation.

Efrat put her backpack on the back of her chair, and set her history folder down on her gray desk. Then she went over to the group where Rotem Uchana was telling about her Passover vacation.

"…So my Aunt was supposed to have been in the hotel where the suicide bomber blew himself up. And we didn't know that she hadn't felt good and so didn't go! So we were really worried, until she called us and told us she was fine and all."

"Wow! What a miracle," Tamar said softly.

"Yes," Rotem nodded her head importantly. "And the *Shabbat* after that she said *Hagomel* in the synagogue – her *Rav* told her to."

The group fell silent for a bit. Then Tamar started telling her story. Efrat didn't really listen and only caught excerpts from it:

"...and then we all went to the Gamba restaurant..."

"...and I found a lovely pink skirt, with blue flowers on the side here, and an orange star..."

"Girls, to your places please." Their homeroom teacher entered the classroom. "Start praying please. I'll write on the board a few names of some of the people wounded over Passover. Please pray for their speedy recovery."

The girls settled in their places, and took out their *siddurim*. Tamar hadn't finished telling Rotem, Hadar and Tali about her vacation and quickly promised to continue in recess. Silence settled over the classroom as they all prayed.

Chapter 8

Several nights later, Efrat sat at her desk in her bedroom. She yawned tiredly. Forget it, she thought. I'm too tired to solve more math problems. On a piece of paper in front of her she had written:

$$X^2 + 5X + 4 = 0$$

$$A = 1$$

$$B = 5$$

$$C = 4$$

$$X = \frac{-5 \pm \sqrt{25-16}}{2}$$

$$X_1 = \frac{-5+3}{2} = \boxed{-1}$$

$$X_2 = \frac{-5-3}{2} = \boxed{-4}$$

She got into bed and lay there, worrying about her math test tomorrow. I know I haven't studied enough for it, she thought worried. And the test will probably be hard, and I'm not prepared – I haven't even gone over my geometry papers! Maybe I'll get up early tomorrow and go over the rest of the material. Maybe if I get up at 5:00 in the morning –

Boom!!!!

The windows all shook and Efrat jumped up from her bed and into her closet where she sat huddled on top of her shoes. My G-d, and I was worried about a stupid math test! was her first scared thought. There were several more booms though none of them were quite as loud as the first one had been.

Efrat's heart beat wildly. Have I been injured, she wondered. Just because I don't feel any pain doesn't mean I haven't been wounded. And that mortar sounded so close, I wouldn't be at all surprised if shrapnel has flown in through my window and into my room and injured me. Her thoughts raced, and she started counting and recounting her fingers and her toes. A huge feeling of relief spread over her as she slowly realized that all her body parts were accounted for, and that she wasn't hurt. "Phew," she sighed in relief.

"Miri, come quick!" Efrat heard her father's voice which rose loudly in the night air. "Two women were walking past our house when the mortars fell. They were injured."

"Oh, no!" Efrat moaned, feeling sick.

"Here, stop here," Efrat heard her father directing the ambulance driver. Several long minutes later, and her parents entered her room. Efrat shakily clambered out of her closet.

"Efrat, did you hear? Three mortars fell around our house: one on the corner and the other two across the street, behind your window," Yoram informed her.

"Yes, I heard." And then she said abruptly, "What does it mean if you're in shock – how do you act?"

Miri looked at her confused. "What do you mean, darling?"

And Efrat told them about jumping into the closet, and counting her fingers and toes.

"Hmm, yes, perhaps you were in shock," Yoram answered, looking at her concerned.

"Well, at any rate I'm fine now. How are the two women?"

"They were taken to the hospital. It's a huge miracle that they were only lightly wounded – considering that they were only a foot away from the mortar that exploded on the corner," Yoram replied.

"And to think that I was worried about a math test," Efrat shook her head in self disgust as she returned to her bed.

She heard Miri's light voice saying to her husband "Yoram,

you should call Yair and tell him that we are all right."

Efrat looked searchingly at her window. There weren't any shrapnel holes in the glass. She turned over and tiredly closed her eyes. *I wonder if I'll have to say Hagomel in the synagogue*, was her last thought before falling asleep.

Chapter 9

Monday, 3 Iyar (April 15)

Dear Mem,

I'm going to give you an update.

It's a bit hard to concentrate with all the shooting going on; it's nonstop!

It happened like this: on my way home from the Ulpana, a bit before the playground, I suddenly see an Arab wheeling a wheelbarrow full of plant trimmings to the garbage. I looked around and saw that no one was outside supervising the Arab worker! I was scared and started envisioning myself dropping my backpack and running... Anyhow, I almost decided on turning back and walking home a different way when, looking up, who do I see, but my father bicycling towards me! I ran to him... After telling Aba how glad I was to see him, he immediately responded: "I didn't want you to walk past the Arab by yourself." Indeed.

Isn't it crazy? During the night the Arabs fire mortars at us, set roadside bombs and try to infiltrate our communities. Yet during the day, we hire them to do our gardening, work in our stores and help us with our household chores! It's crazy. Where is the second Aliya idealism of 'conquering the guard and the work'? They tried to 'conquer' the guard and the work from the Arabs and had a tough time of it. Well, the 'guard' is in Jewish hands, but the 'work' seems to have returned to the Arab hands – the way it was before the second Aliya.

Today Lipaz Cohen came over in order to study with me for our Literature test next week. It went well: we learned three songs and two short stories. Studying for a test with Lipaz is good for me, since I have to explain everything about twice and then when she understands it she goes over it out loud, so I can correct her if need be. In other words, when I study with her I go over the material thrice!

Last night, Aba, Yair (he comes home from Yeshiva every Tuesday night now) and I took flashlights and a can and went toad hunting. It's a strange indescribable feeling to be walking in the dark, between the gray hothouses, with the bright stars above, good company (!) and shooting in the background. The family who own the small swimming pool in Gadid from which we heard the toads croaking, were very friendly as was their small black dog. Sadly, we didn't see any toads though we heard them very loudly.

Good night,
Efrat.

~~~

Several days later, to Efrat's delight, the town council of Neve Dekalim decided not to allow any Arabs into the community.

"*Aba*, how come Neve Dekalim voted not to allow Arabs into the community and yet Gadid and other *moshavim* didn't pass a similar vote?"

"Simple. It's because Neve Dekalim isn't an agricultural community; it's a town not a *moshav*."

"What does that mean?"

"It means that Neve Dekalim isn't dependent upon Arabs working in their hot houses – Neve Dekalim doesn't have hothouses. The hothouses I work in are in B'dolach which is a *moshav*."

"Neve Dekalim doesn't have Arabs anymore, but it has other foreign workers: Chinese, Thais, Philippines… Can't the *moshavim* only hire those and not Arabs?"

"Good question, Effie. And the reasons that they can't are because: (1) hiring Arabs is a lot cheaper. (2) there aren't enough Chinese and Thai workers."

"Ah, I see. What a shame! Do *you* work with Arabs?" Efrat asked her father bluntly and a bit accusingly.

"Yes, Efrat. I do. I don't have much of a choice; if I'm going to work in hothouses checking vegetables for insects then I'm going to be around Arabs. It isn't very pleasant and it isn't the safest thing

The hothouses

in the world but that's just how it is. Whenever my boss can find Jews who are willing to work in hothouses, he hires them. But the Jews who are willing to work in hothouses are few. I think they'd rather collect unemployment than work long hours in the hothouses during the summer…"

"I'm sorry you have to work in a situation that isn't very safe, *Aba*. Even though I'm sure you take protective measures."

Yoram shrugged. "I never work by myself; I'm always with my partner. It's safer that way; less risk of being stabbed in the back."

"Goodness! Has that ever happened, has an Arab ever stabbed a Jew in the back?"

Yoram nodded, soberly. "I'm afraid so. I know a case, it happened a while ago. A fellow in Gadid always drove the Arabs he hired to and from work. Trusted 'em. Had them for more than

seven years. One day, he was driving them and one of his 'loyal' Arabs took out a knife and stabbed him in the back."

"Ouch!"

"No kidding, Effie. Well, that's it. I've finished trimming all the trees. Time to pick up the trimmings and add them to the pile across the street. Do you want to help, Effie?"

"What? No Arabs to do it for us?! Just kidding, *Aba*, of course I'll help!"

A cool spring evening breeze blows Efrat's wavy brown hair backwards and around her shoulders as she uses the green rake to gather the cut branches into a tidy pile. Together she and her father gather the trimmings into old white buckets and dump the cuttings across the street on the sand.

"The pile of trimmings is getting big, *Aba*," Efrat commented after they'd dumped the last bucket of trimmings onto the pile.

"Yes it is. In a few more days – after I mow the lawn, I'll burn it all up."

Efrat nodded, and Yoram carried the buckets back to the house.

Chapter 10

6 Iyar (April 29)

Dear Mem,

Well, yesterday was Israel's Independence Day. I had a great time; in the night we walked down to the town center. More people selling candy and such stuff than any other year yet. We stayed to dance a bit, and then Yair and I walked back home. At 11:00 p.m. were the first batch of fireworks and they weren't very impressive. Ima and Aba came home soon after and we went to bed. At midnight I was awakened by what I thought was a close mortar, but what Yair shouted was fireworks. Sure enough! They were gorgeous! Yair and I rushed outside and stood watching them burst against the dark night sky. Like Aba had feared, some mortars did fall at the same time that the fireworks were exploding, and all those still celebrating in the town center were told to go into protected areas. Ten minutes later they were allowed out.

The following morning, we all woke up late, got dressed wearing blue and white clothes and prayed – adding Hallel of course. After a festive breakfast we prepared to go walk along the beaches until Tel Katifa. Yair and I were about to go when Ima insisted we both wear hats. Yair adamantly refused, and sadly I prepared to go without him when happily Yair changed his mind and together we walked down to the gate of Neve Dekalim. It took us a long time to catch a ride down to the beach, but we finally did and got there O.K.

Some booths were set up at which people were selling hats and shirts, but they weren't quite what we wanted so in the end we didn't buy any.

We set out walking along the beach. Oh! The sea and the sky! Lovely. Yair caught a crab, goofed around...We climbed some cliffs, collected a few seashells, played Frisbee and had a lot of fun.

Finally we got to Tel Katifa, got some free kites and cotton candy, walked around the small seaside community and then started heading back along the beaches to Neve Dekalim. When we arrived at the beach parking lot, our elderly neighbors spotted us and gave as a ride "until our door." Very nice.

Back home we did a cook out – hot dogs and potatoes on a grill. The chef was Yair; the food turned out good.

Efrat.

~~~

"Hey, Efrat. Let's go for a walk."

"O.K. Yair. Where to?"

"I don't know," Yair shrugged. "Around."

Efrat closed her book, walked to her room and placed the book on her desk, closed her bedroom door and joined her brother. They set out the front door and into the bright Tamuz (June) sunshine.

"Well, Efrat, another school year has passed," Yair remarked happily.

"It really sped by, didn't it?" Efrat commented a bit glumly.

"You bet it did! I was talking to *Aba* yesterday about how this school year has seemed to finish quicker than others, and at first he said that every year it seems that way. But then he added that this year has been a very difficult one – living as we have from one terror attack to another, and that perhaps that has made it seem to pass quicker."

"Yes, a lot of Jews have been killed this year and many have been wounded."

"And we've been on the front lines!" Yair put in excitedly. "Three mortars fell right around our house, and whatever neighborhood you walk in around Neve Dekalim you can find mortar holes and shrapnel marks."

"Yes," Efrat agreed. "But the government fixes the damage so quickly that it hardly seems that anything has happened."

"Explain, please," Yair requested, as he picked a leaf off an oleander hedge they were walking next to.

"Well, a mortar falls. Two minutes later we're told over the loudspeakers: 'Residents of Neve Dekalim, good evening. Please enter protected areas.' Then, about half an hour later we're told over the loudspeakers: 'Residents of Neve Dekalim, back to routine. I repeat, residents…' and then what do we do?"

"We rush to where the mortars fell," Yair said grinning. "We play tourists – going to the new attraction and looking at the damage and hunting for souvenirs!"

"Right. And, amazingly, no one is hurt but there is a lot of damage."

"Sure. Windows cracked, roof tiles missing, a big hole wherever the mortar landed…" Yair trailed off.

"Precisely," Efrat conceded. "But go back two days later and what do you see?" She answered her own question: "The hole has been filled, the broken glass replaced, the blinds with shrapnel holes have been changed, the roof mended… like nothing ever happened!"

"Well, nothing really has happened. I mean," he added quickly, "I don't like mortars falling but as long as no one is hurt and the damage is fixed…"

"Yair," Efrat said soberly, "we can't rely on miracles. Before vacation started we had this long speech from the *Rav* – you know talking about this past year and advice for the vacation… and one of the things he stressed was precisely that: that we can't rely on miracles. That just because most of the mortars haven't injured anyone doesn't mean that it'll always be like that!"

"He's right," Yair agreed. "Hey, remember in the beginning? In the beginning, we'd get so scared just from hearing shooting! Now no one pays attention to the shooting. And no one even pays attention to mortars falling, unless the mortar happened to have fallen close."

Efrat and Yair were silent for a bit. Yair bent down, plucked a yellow flower from its light green stem and started shredding it petal by petal.

Efrat broke the silence. "Yair, do you think next year will be like this too?"

"I've an idea that stuff will continue pretty much the same," Yair replied. "I mean, why shouldn't it?" he asked, warming up to the subject. "The Arabs can shoot at us, bomb us at night and then come work in most of our hothouses during the day. And they know that the army will warn them half an hour before bombing some buildings that the Arabs fired mortars from. So why should they stop?"

"You know, Yair, when there's a big suicide bombing in Jerusalem or Netanya or Haifa, the country goes on high alert and there's an army response. Perhaps not an adequate army response, but at least some response. Yet when the Arabs attack us here, there isn't even that response! Why is the government abandoning us like this?"

Yair's face darkened with anger, before he managed to shrug it off and grin humorlessly. "I don't know, Effie. I can only assume that, like us, the government has gotten used to Gush Katif being bombed. And since it's pretty rare that a Gush Katif resident gets injured, the government ignores it," Yair's voice rose. "How can we blame the government when we, the ones being bombed, don't protest? Do you think the residents of Tel Aviv would put up with this? D'you think the people of any normal city would put up with this?!"

"Good point, Yair," Efrat replied thoughtfully. "O.K. then, I've got a question: why **do** we put up with it?"

"It's simple, Efrat. Because we aren't normal."

"Speak for yourself," Efrat retorted cheerfully and gave her brother a shove.

They turned in at a playground and sat down on the swings.

"Ah," Efrat sighed contently. "Blue skies, a blue sea, golden sand dunes and summer vacation here again. What more could one want?"

Some gunshots crackled in the distance, but Yair and Efrat ignored them and kept on swinging. Up and down, up and down under the clear summer sky.

"Shall a shofar be sounded in the city, and the people not be afraid? The lion has roared, who will not fear?" [Amos 3: 6, 8.]

Chapter 11

Some mornings later and Efrat returned from taking Rufus on a walk only to find her brother and her parents in the midst of a heated argument.

"I said no! And I'm not changing my mind," Yoram said sternly. "It's dangerous!"

"But *Aba*!" Yair pleaded, "All the kids have live bullets! What's dangerous about them? What?"

"They could go off by accident, Yair, you know that; if they're dropped on the floor, if they get heated up too much they could go off. Anyhow, you heard your father, he said no," Miri said in a sharp voice which her children rarely heard her use.

Efrat sat down quietly by Yair and didn't say a word.

"But I won't drop them and they won't get overheated!" Yair pleaded. "I'll be very careful – I'm not a baby."

"No!" Yoram thundered. "And that's final. Stop arguing."

Yair quickly stood up and left the house. Efrat followed him. They walked up the hill in silence.

"Effie, what is Ima's and Aba's problem?"

"Oh, come on, Yair. You know they are right!"

"It's a shame. I'd wanted to do experiments like my friends do."

"Hmm, what?"

"You know, wrap gun powder in tape and then light it. Things like that. Experiments."

"Yair! That is precisely why *Aba* and *Ima* say it's dangerous to have live ammunition. And they won't let you keep an ammunition collection at all if you plan to play around with it."

"I know," Yair sighed regretfully. "Fine, I won't."

"I hope not," Efrat said shortly. "Where are we headed to?"

"Last night some friends of mine gave them to me – they had a

58

lot and agreed to give me some."

"Cool! What type?"

"MG. They are really big. *No* comparison to an M16. And the bullets come in two colors: regular and red tracer MGs."

"So where are they?"

"I buried them by the fence of Gadid, 'cause they are live and I figured *Ima* and *Aba* wouldn't let me bring live bullets home," Yair smiled, pleased with himself.

The fence of Gadid

Efrat shook her head. "Yair, you are hopeless! So what are you going to do with them? They are live!"

Yair shrugged, "I'll have to trade most of them with friends. They'll give me dead stuff in exchange – hey, maybe I'll try and trade for a flare including the parachute; we don't have many of those, only the one that *Aba* brought home that one of the Arab hothouse workers had found in B'dolach and given to him."

"Good idea," Efrat agreed. "But," she added keenly, "I noticed you said you would trade *most* of them. In other words, there are some live bullets that you do not plan to trade!"

Yair laughed. "You're pretty sharp, Effie. Careful," he teased her, "or you'll get so sharp you'll cut yourself."

"Come on!" Efrat persisted. "What are you planning to do

with the remaining live MG bullets?"

"Watch and you'll see," Yair said impatiently for they had now reached the fence separating the community of Neve Dekalim from the community of Gadid. Yair turned left and started walking along side the fence on the Gadid side. Efrat walked beside him closely. Yair suddenly stopped her. "Here, see this small bush?" Without waiting for a reply he continued, "From here we count ten fence poles and then we dig. They aren't buried deep."

Efrat nodded and her brown eyes twinkled. "Really, Yair, you've been reading too many pirate stories."

"Nah, just seen Treasure Island one too many times," Yair joked.

Together they counted ten fence poles and then sat down on the warm golden sand and started digging.

"Here," Yair said after about two minutes. "I feel metal."

Efrat stopped digging and brushed the sand from her hands. Yair steadily cleared the sand away and started lifting MG bullets from the shallow hole. Efrat started counting them: "one, two, three...five..."

"There should be twenty five of them," Yair commented without stopping from lifting the bullets out, shaking the sand off of them and handing them to Efrat."

"...twenty four, twenty five," Efrat finished counting.

"Right," Yair said, pulling a plastic bag out from a pant pocket. "Here, put them in the bag." Yair picked out five bullets, and Efrat carefully put the rest in the bag.

"O.K. This bag of twenty bullets I'll trade. But these five I will open up so that they won't be live anymore."

"You can do that?" Efrat asked, impressed.

"Sure. It's easy. All we need is a sidewalk curb that is cracked and a plastic container for the gun powder."

They started walking back the way they had come. Soon they had reached the street and turned back in the direction of their house. Yair was carefully studying the gray sidewalk curbs while Efrat was looking at the sea, watching the white caps disappear in the deep blue water. Five spur winged plovers flew over head coasting gracefully on currents of air. Their black and white spurred wings stood out sharply against the light blue sky. They trilled sharply and alighted carefully on the bare sand.

"Efrat, stop daydreaming, would you please?" Yair was standing still next to a narrow crack that ran along a sidewalk curb. He handed her a small plastic container and four bullets. The remaining bullet he held tightly in his hand and wedged into the sidewalk curb crack. He twisted the bullet from side to side until the bullet worked loose from the shell. Efrat held the container carefully as he poured the dark gray gun powder into the container. Then he put both parts of the bullet in his pocket and Efrat handed him another MG bullet. When they had finished making the live ammunition harmless, they buried the bag with the twenty live bullets under the brown fallen leaves around the thick silvery stem of a large nearby acacia tree. Yair stuck a stick in the leaves so that he'd be able to find the place easily.

Efrat chuckled. "Just think, Yair, we have our own 'slik'"

Yair nodded. "Hey, that is right! Just like the Jews in the time of the British had to hide their ammunition in secret places called 'sliks' we're also hiding ammunition."

Efrat was studying the plastic container she still held in her hand. "Wow, that was a lot of gunpowder in those bullets."

"Sure," Yair agreed. "'Cause they are large bullets."

And feeling slightly guilty they returned home.

Chapter 12

12 Tamuz (June 22)

Dear Mem,

What a day I had yesterday! Ima took Yair to a dental appointment and then to shop for a new pair of sandals for him. I did a few more of the trigonometry problems our math teacher gave us to do during summer vacation and then went across the street to my neighbor's house to water her garden. While watering the honeysuckle vines, I noticed a small brown head of a chameleon! I quickly turned the water off, rushed back to the honeysuckle and attempted to find it. I didn't succeed. So after looking and looking through the leaves and branches, I turned the water back on and drenched the area. I then bent over the vines looking again and listening carefully. But no luck! So I went around the vines, and there on the other side I found it quickly and, grabbing it's tail, I scooped it into the palm of my hand and ran home with it, full of suppressed excitement. I rushed in the house, calling for Aba. I found him at his desk. Aba was surprised by how small the chameleon was... I decided to keep it – it was soooo cute! Aba quickly found a glass jar that would be perfect to keep it in. So I rubbed the sticker off the jar and placed it outside to dry. Aba took the cap off the jar and thought that a piece of screen netting fastened with rubber bands would make the best top for it. He also thought that putting soil would work better than sand, because I wanted to put some plants into the jar. That being decided, we "took time by the fetlock," snatched a large scissors and a bucket and walked up the hill to Gadid.

We had just passed through the gate of Gadid when Aba noticed some object a few meters away from the sidewalk on which we were walking, and asked me what the object was.

Well, I walked off the sidewalk and onto the sand to get a better look. Casually I asked Aba who had joined me, "mortar?" And just as casually Aba answered "Nope. Rocket – kassam."

Isn't it amazing? I'd often wondered this past year how I would react if I came across a live mortar or kassam... And yet here Aba and I had actually come across a live kassam and we were behaving like two calm scientists!

We observed that about a foot of it was protruding from the ground, it's fins reaching up to the sky. It looked, in my opinion, rather like something out of a science fiction movie. Aba was worried that the Thais who lived across the street might set it off by accident. So he started to slowly and loudly explain to them in easy Hebrew that this was a very dangerous object here, that if touched it might 'boom' (accompanied with hand gestures of something exploding).

Aba was friendly with the Rav Shatz – the man in charge of Gadid security, but didn't know his phone number. However, since we knew where he lived in Gadid, we started walking towards his house. Luckily, after only walking a short distance, a security car passed us and Aba flagged it down. It was Mr. Mor and Aba quickly told him the story. Mr. Mor turned his car around and roared off – going past where the kassam was. So...we started running after him, calling him to stop (a bit embarrassing actually; all the workers from Thailand (Thais) were standing by the kassam and watching us curiously). Mr. Mor saw us in the mirror and drove back. We showed him the unexploded rocket and he assured us that everything would be all right "yehiyeh be'seder."

Having alerted the security people, Aba and I made our way through the throng of silent, curious Thais and continued on our way to the hothouses to get potting soil and netting.

Ima called Aba to tell him the results of Yair's dentist appointment (one cavity), and Aba and I got the dirt and the netting. When I asked Aba why he hadn't said anything to Ima about the kassam rocket we had just found, he answered: "There are some things it isn't wise to tell over the phone." He is right, I suppose.

On the way back home we passed where the rocket was. A lot of security jeeps were pulling up and Aba explained to them that he was the one who had found the rocket. Hmm, no prize given to the finder…

Back at home we hosed the netting down and cut it to the right size. We added the potting soil to the jar, put in a pronged stick, a smooth white stone and a leaf. Lastly we gently placed the small baby chameleon inside. Perfect!

I've placed the jar on my dresser's top shelf, by the window so it'll get sunlight. It really looks great. Yair's going to be jealous…

Ima called to say she and Yair were taking a long time finding a pair of sandals that Yair liked, and that I should make dinner. So I made pizza. And after dinner I went back over to my neighbor's house to finish watering.

Efrat.

Chapter 13

That *Shabbat*, in the middle of the hot summer month of Tamuz (July), Yoram and Yair returned from the synagogue *Shabbat* eve accompanied by a young good looking soldier.

"You guys are late, what took you so long?" Efrat asked as she ran to greet them. "Oops," she stopped short as she noticed the guest. She blushed with embarrassment and absentmindedly brushed back a lock of her soft brown wavy hair. Miri came and joined her, and Efrat smelled the scent of her mother's flowery perfume.

"We're home later than usual 'cause the chazzan picked a really slow melody for *Lecha Dodi*," Yair grumbled. "I don't know why he did it, drove half the congregation nuts."

The soldiers bright gray eyes twinkled, "oh, it wasn't that bad," he commented politely.

Yoram explained to Miri "this is Dror Alit. He's serving in this area and didn't have where to eat this *Shabbat*. So I invited him for the evening meal."

"Otherwise he'd be stuck eating a *Shabbat* meal out of tins!" Yair put in.

Miri smiled graciously, "you're very welcome to join us at our *Shabbat* table," she said warmly. "Generally Yoram doesn't have a chance to invite soldiers home for a meal; they've already been invited to other families!"

Dror grinned, "Well, quite a number of my unit are religious. So whoever could, went to the synagogue; we must have been about twenty men and we split up in the different synagogues."

"And there was an empty seat by Yair and me – because the Levi family went away this *Shabbat* to visit their cousins in Shiloh – so Dror sat by me and I immediately invited him home for dinner." Yoram finished explaining and grinned, pleased with himself.

"O.K. enough talking," Yair cut in. "Let's talk after we eat."

They all laughed and walked inside the house.

The dining room was very bright and cheery. In honor of *Shabbat*, a pure white tablecloth was on the table, the Yefets' best dishes and silverware adorned the table, scarlet napkins were folded neatly beside the white plates resting beneath the heavy shining silverware, and a graceful vase full of fresh roses and dark green foliage resided in the center of the table. The *Shabbat* candles that Miri and Efrat had lit right before Yoram and Yair had left for *Shul* were still burning bright, though the candles were already halfway melted; the wax having oozed out from under the burning flame and drifted down the candle's stiff white sides.

Dror glanced around the living room and a soft look stole into his keen gray eyes. He carefully removed his M16 that was strapped over his shoulder and across his back, and leaned it against the wall. Rufus came trotting over to sniff the stranger. Dror was delighted, "You have a very cute dog," and pet Rufus' fluffy fur. The Yefet family laughed as Rufus quickly lost interest and trotted away.

"He doesn't like much attention, Rufus doesn't," Yoram chuckled. "Not like Beauty. Beauty is outside in her pen, but she'll be delighted to be pet. No such thing as too much attention for Beauty."

Yair nodded in agreement.

They all sat down around the table; Yoram at one end with Dror on his right and Yair on his left. Efrat sat next to Yair and Miri sat at the other end of the table – opposite Yoram.

Yoram started singing *Shalom Aleichem* and they all joined in. The soldier Dror joined in a bit shyly and they couldn't hear his voice at all during the first stanza. But in the second stanza Dror seemed to have forgotten his strangeness and joined in heartily. His deep voice was very pleasant to listen to:

"...*Borchuni l'shalom malchay*
Hashalom malchay elyon,
Mimelech malchay hamelachim
Hakadosh baruch hu.

Tzayt'chem l'shalom malchay
Hashalom malchay elyon,

Mimelech malchay hamelachim
Hakadosh baruch hu."

They finished singing the last two verses:
"...Bless me with peace, messengers of peace, messengers of the Most High, of the supreme King of Kings, the Holy One, Blessed be He.

"And may your departure be in peace, messengers of peace, messengers of the Most High, of the supreme King of Kings, the Holy One, blessed be He."

Yoram looked affectionately at his wife as they sang Eshet Chayil (A Woman of Valor) and Miri smiled, pleased.

Then first Efrat and then Yair went to Yoram for a blessing. Yoram placed his right hand on Efrat's head: "May G-d make you like Sarah, Rivka, Rachel and Leah. May the Lord bless you and watch over you. May the Lord shine His face towards you and show you favor. May the Lord be favorably disposed towards you and may He grant you peace."

"Amen!" Miri, Yair and Dror answered and Efrat went over to her mother to receive a hug and a whispered "May you know right from wrong and choose right." Efrat kissed her mother and sat back in her seat.

Yoram put his right hand on Yair's head. "Hey, you've grown!" He teased Yair, "look I have to stretch my arm."

Yair grinned. "Hey, *Aba*, I'll be taller than you soon!"

Yoram chuckled "taller – maybe. But not stronger." And he gave Yair his blessing: "May G-d make you like Ephraim and Menashe. May the Lord bless you and watch over you. May the Lord shine his face towards you and show you favor. May the Lord be favorably disposed towards you and may He grant you peace." Yair then embraced his mother and received her whispered "May you know..."

They all pushed their chairs back and stood for *Kiddush*. Efrat hurried to get the bottle of Hebron sweet red wine, her father's favorite *Kiddush* wine. They filled their cups and raised them and Yoram recited the *Kiddush* over his special silver goblet filled with ruby red wine just like his fathers had done before him for the past several thousand years. "Vai – hi erev vai – hi voker yom hashishi…" ("And it was evening and it was morning the sixth day…") Yoram intoned in a melodious tone.

Efrat stood erectly, her wavy brown hair falling onto her fancy white *Shabbat* shirt, her polished black shoes peeping out from under the lacy hem of her purple skirt with tiny white flowers dotted over it. Her necklace sparkled in the light as she turned her head to gaze at her father standing proudly in his ironed white *Shabbat* shirt and dark blue pants holding his silver *Kiddush* wine cup in one hand and his siddur in the other. Her gaze swept on to Yair, who really was nearly her father's height. He was holding his cup very steady lest the wine drop onto his white *Shabbat* shirt (his top collar button was unfastened) or light brown pants. Miri looked lovely. She was wearing a satin white shirt under a flowing rose colored sleeveless dress. The stone on her necklace just matched the shade of her dress. Yoram had given her that necklace as a present on their past anniversary.

Discretely, Efrat gazed at the soldier. Dror was standing erectly; his head up, his back straight and his shoulders back. His keen gray eyes were shining, and Efrat wondered how long it had been since he had last heard *Kiddush* recited in a home. Efrat looked at Dror again. He was very handsome and a bit taller than her father.

"…*Baruch atah ado – noy, mikadaysh hashabbat*" ("…Blessed are you O Lord who sanctifies the *Shabbat*"). Yoram finished reciting *Kiddush*, and they all sat down and drank the wine.

It was only after *Hamotzei*, the blessing over the bread, that they started with the *Shabbat* meal Miri had prepared; chicken, rice, potato kugel and salads. Then the conversation started.

"So, Dror, where are you from?" Yoram asked as he took a bite of potato kugel.

Dror's smile lit up his face. "I'm from Kiryat Arba."

"Ah," Yoram nodded his head. "We have many good friends there."

"Some friends of mine learn at the *Yeshiva* there," Yair confessed, "but I decided to go here to the Katif Yeshiva."

Dror looked up with interest sparked in his gray eyes. "So you go to the Katif Yeshiva. And your sister?"

Efrat smiled, "I go to the *Ulpana* here – Ulpanat Neve Dekalim."

Dror smiled back, "ah, I know the *Rav* that heads it. I like him."

"Yes," Efrat agreed. "He is very good and is, in my opinion, the best *Rav* the *Ulpana* has had yet."

Dror continued "so you two study here in the Gush, and you," turning to Yoram, "you work in the Gush?"

"Correct," Yoram replied. "I check a lot of hothouses in B'dolach. This season I'm mainly checking lettuce and green onions."

"Yes," Miri put in softly, "this is where we live, this is where our lives are."

A comfortable silence fell on the room. It was broken simultaneously by distant rapid gunfire, and by Dror looking up from his plate and staying steadily "we soldiers do our best so you all can continue your everyday lives here."

"Oh, we don't blame the soldiers," Yair said quickly. "We blame the government."

Dror smiled wearily, "I'm glad to hear that. The government and the Supreme Court force us to watch idly as the Arabs shoot mortars at your settlements. We can't shoot the Arabs who are firing the missiles since it's done quickly and they are fond of surrounding themselves with children as they fire the mortars. And we can't even destroy the tall buildings they fire from without the Supreme Court approving the operation. But it takes a long time to get the court's approval since they are left wing and the Arabs and left wing organizations in Israel do all they can to sway the court not to give the approval. And if the court does approve demolishing the building, it's nearly always contested."

"Crazy," Efrat remarked.

"Oh, nothing's changed," Yoram commented. "Our leaders have always preferred Havlaga – restraint over Tguva – action."

And as Efrat and Yair looked at their father questionably, Dror explained: "Your father's 100% right. Back in 1936 when Israel was still 'Palestine', the Arabs started rioting and killing Jews. The Jews were divided as to how to respond: Havlaga or Tguva. Havlaga meant not attacking the Arabs until they attacked us. In other words, attacking only as a defense after having been attacked, and to do everything so as not injure innocent Arabs – even at the expense of Jewish lives. On the other hand, Tguva meant not waiting until the Arabs attacked you; rather to attack the Arabs before hand – and if Arabs were killed in the process then so be it, better them than Jews. Well, our leadership has always preferred Havlaga over Tguva."

Again silence fell over the room. This time Miri broke it by asking Yair to talk about the weekly Torah reading.

"Right," Yair said importantly. "Just a second, let me remember what we learned at *Yeshiva*." He was silent a few minutes, deep in thought. Suddenly he grinned, "O.K. I remember. This week's Torah reading is called Pinchas. Pinchas killed Zimri who was the head of the tribe of Shimon, and right afterwards Pinchas was rewarded by *Hashem* giving him the covenant of peace. Now this seems strange – what's peaceful about killing a man, even if that man had sinned badly?" Yair paused here and looked around the table, but as no one seemed about to answer, he continued, "the answer is that we have a warped sense of the concept 'peace.' According to the Torah, as we learn from this issue with Pinchas, the Torah's way of bringing peace is by making the world a better place, and that is done by uprooting evil and evil doers from the world. There is no coexistence between good and evil or between good people and bad people. *Hashem* demands of the good people, the righteous, that they burn out the evil from the world – 'and you shall burn out the evil from thy midst,' for only thus will peace reign in the world. There are two stages in order to bring peace: first 'depart from evil' and then 'and do good' – first 'sur mi ra' and only afterwards 've aseh tov.' And Pinchas was worthy of the covenant of peace because he arose and eradicated the evil."

Yair finished and they all clapped their hands.

Dror chuckled. "I like your policy of peace."

"So do I," Yoram agreed. "I never thought about it that way before. But it makes sense."

"Well," Miri said. "If we're all done eating, let's start singing."

"We're done," Efrat said, glancing around the table. "What song shall we start with?"

"How about Bar Yochai?" Miri suggested.

"Yair, go get the *zmironim*," Yoram requested.

So Yair got the songbooks and they all started singing.

"Stop banging on the table, Yair," Yoram said sternly.

"Why, it sounds nice?" Miri asked.

"I want to be able to hear if any mortars fall," Yoram explained.

They all laughed, but Yair quickly stopped tapping on the table in time to the tune.

"Hate the evil, and love the good, and establish justice in the gate: it may be that the Lord G-d of Hosts will be gracious to the remnant of Yosef." [Amos 5: 15.]

Chapter 14

"Stop playing your clarinet, and listen to me please," Efrat said as she entered Yair's room.

"What's the matter?" Yair asked, lowering his shiny black clarinet.

"Oh, I don't know," Efrat shrugged her shoulders. "It's just that we return to school tomorrow. I start twelfth grade and you're going to start tenth grade."

"You're lucky, Efrat. It's your last year."

Efrat smiled sadly. "Oh, I don't know," she said yet again. "I'll be sad to finish the *Ulpana*."

"Sad?" Yair echoed her in shock.

"Yes, sad. I've got a feeling that this coming year is going to be a really difficult year."

"Well, you do have a lot of bagruts (Israel matriculation exams)."

"No, no," Efrat laughed. "I'm not concerned study wise."

"Then what are you worried about?" Yair asked his sister, a bit bemused.

Efrat sighed. "I enjoy the *Ulpana*. I'm, well, attached to the *Rav* and the staff…and I'll be sorry to leave them. Also, I'm going to have to find a place to do National Service."

Yair nodded, suddenly thoughtful. "Well, I need to get my backpack ready for tomorrow."

Efrat sighed, then nodded "Yes, me too."

"Hey, Effie, you really seem depressed."

Efrat shrugged, "I'm in a bad mood."

"It's not like you to be depressed. And I've got a feeling you haven't told me what's really bothering you," Yair said shrewdly.

Efrat raised an eyebrow.

"Oh yes," Yair continued. "Just being worried about finding a

National Service position, and being sad to leave the *Ulpana* wouldn't make you feel so blue!"

Efrat smiled and said, "You know me too well." She was silent for a few minutes as she toyed with the zipper of Yair's backpack. Yair waited patiently, taking his clarinet apart and drying the pieces before placing them in their snug velvet compartments. "I suppose," she said finally, "that I'm depressed because I was thinking of all the terror attacks lately. And then I started thinking about life and death. Well, mainly about death."

Yair whistled softly. "Tough subject," he said casually.

"I'm being serious!" Efrat protested, upset since her brother seemed to be taking it lightly.

"So am I," Yair assured her. "You just surprised me, that's all."

Reassured, Efrat explained "you see, I was thinking about all the mortars that have fallen..."

"4,692 according to a website listing," Yair put in.

"Right. And they land everywhere at any time of the day or the night. We could get killed very easily or wounded badly!"

"You're right. It's like what we said when those three mortars fell around our house – that we had known all along that it was only a matter of time before some mortars fell close to our house."

"Yair," Efrat said urgently, "how do you deal with the knowledge that any day you could be injured or killed, G-d forbid, by a mortar?"

Yair rubbed his large hand along the curve of his firm jaw, thinking deeply all the while. "It's like this," he finally said, "like the sages say, man is born against his will and he also dies against his will. It isn't up to us – so why worry about what you don't control? Also," he continued, "even with all the terror attacks, the number one cause of death in Israel is still from car accidents!"

At that Efrat grinned weakly, "So I'm worrying about the wrong thing, hmm."

Yair continued speaking, "We do our best. We take the safety measures we can; we get inside a protected area when mortars fall, we ride in armored buses until we pass the Kissufim Junction, *Ima* and *Aba* try not to travel together in case of a roadside bomb or shooting or a suicide bomber... Anyhow, we do our best. After that, it's out of our hands."

"Yes," Efrat agreed. "Every place has its dangers. We try to protect ourselves, and once we've done that then there is no point worrying; we know we've done our best, and *Hashem* controls it."

Yair headed out of his bedroom and into the living room. He searched the shelves, found the book he was looking for and brought it to Efrat. "Remember when you made me read this?"

Efrat looked at the book. Her face relaxed into a warm smile, *Gidi – And The Campaign To Expel The British From Israel* by Yosef Evron. "Oh yes, an excellent book."

"Well, you seem to have forgotten something in it," Yair chuckled. That's not like you, Effie."

Efrat looked chagrined.

Yair flipped through the pages. "Here, pages 356 – 357."

Efrat took the book.

"Get comfortable, it's a bit long," Yair suggested.

Efrat sat down on Yair's bed and started reading:

> Once in a time of distress, I came to pour my heart before him. He listened to me patiently, and when I finished speaking, he gave me a long look and said in his quiet voice, and the things he said then still echo in my ears and will continue to follow me for many days. 'Chaim' – he said – 'we all live miraculously. I am not a fatalist in the full meaning of the word, but I believe, that what is supposed to happen, is almost impossible to prevent. These are our lives and this is the fate we chose from our own free will. Calm down – and keep stepping forwards in the path you've chosen. We must continue, as long as it depends on us, towards the goal that we've set for ourselves. And beyond that – what must happen – will happen anyway.'

Efrat smiled. Good for you, Yair, she thought to herself. She kept on reading:

> In these words, which were said in a quiet and calm tone, Amichai Feiglin [Gidi] had actually given voice to his whole life philosophy, according to which he acted from the dawn of his youth and all the length of his turbulent life; in the daring attacks that he planned and executed in the relentless struggle against the British during the years 1944 – 1948, as he stepped erectly forwards, sticking to the goal, without fear, without hesitation – until the hand of fate cruelly overtook him in 1978 in a disastrous car acci-

dent, in which he lost his life together with his wife, Tziporah, who had escorted him loyally from the days of the underground until the tragic end. [Translated from the Hebrew by Shifra Shomron]

"Hmm," Efrat said out loud. "Brilliant interview! Everyone in Gush Katif, nay – in all of Israel, should read it."

Yair shrugged. "I don't generally remember stuff I read, but that part had stuck in my mind."

"I am very glad it did," Efrat said emphatically.

"Feel better, Effie?" Yair asked anxiously.

"Yes, I do," Efrat replied. "Thank you, you've been a huge help."

"No problem. Hey, remember what *Ima* and *Aba* said when mortars first started falling in Neve Dekalim, and they were wondering if perhaps we should move from here?"

"Oh, yes I remember. They said that living here in Gush Katif is a big mitzvah – settling the land. And that if we didn't stay here, then the Arabs would grab it. And that if we leave Gush Katif because the Arabs are attacking us, then we might as well leave Israel because the Arabs will attack us wherever and whenever they can. But since this is our land and *Hashem* commanded us to live in it, we'll just have to do our best and face the dangers."

"Exactly. Good memory," Yair complimented her.

Efrat rose.

"Where are you going?" Yair asked, surprised.

Efrat paused in the doorway, "I need to get my backpack ready for school tomorrow," she said cheerfully.

Yair winked. "Oh, yeah, me too."

"I will bear the indignation of the Lord, because I have sinned against Him, until He plead my cause, and execute judgment for me; He will bring me forth to the light, and I shall behold His righteousness. Then my enemy shall see it, and shame shall cover her; who said to me, Where is the Lord thy G-d? My eyes shall behold her; now she shall be trodden down as the mire of the streets." [Micha 7: 9-10.]

Chapter 15

Efrat started twelfth grade. It was quite a change to suddenly become the grade all the other, younger, grades looked up to; as the oldest students in the school they set the example.

Classes were a bit different; they didn't have Hebrew grammar or Literature anymore, biology became more intensive and they had a new class, citizenship, which was very boring. In fact, a lot of girls skipped coming to citizenship class or dozed through it. Efrat, however, considered the class important and took very good notes. The only sign of her dislike of the subject was the fact that she used a *black* double ringed folder and a *black* pen. Very subtle and symbolic.

Several girls had gotten their driver licenses over the summer vacation. The twelfth grade started thinking about the play they would perform in the beginning of the month of Adar (March) – the week in which they would run the *Ulpana*. Other than that, little had changed and the twelfth grade settled into the routine of classes, tests and social activities.

The High Holidays passed. Efrat's discomfort at seeing that once again the new moon of the New Year was surrounded by a distinct red haze, was soon forgotten by the more important worry of keeping up with the demanding load of schoolwork.

The month of Tishrei (October) passed. In biology class Efrat and her two teammates Hadar and Merav started planning the experiment they would conduct for their Biology project.

And before they realized it, the 22nd of Cheshvan (November 20th) was upon them; the memorial date for their beloved teacher Miriam who had been killed by Arabs. The *Ulpana* had of course prepared a big ceremony for the tragic date and on that day, the 22nd of Cheshvan, all the students and the staff gathered in the large hall. A big picture showing Miriam's smiling face had been hung up, the tables had been pushed to the side and the chairs had been neatly set in rows. Several girls from Efrat's grade had prepared poems and short speeches. One grade at the *Ulpana* had actually composed a song.

Rather silently, without the usual chatter that would have normally accompanied an *Ulpana* gathering, the girls sat down according to grades and the teachers sat down among the students.

The *Rav* walked up to the front of the hall. Looking at the girls he said: "Not all of you have had the privilege of knowing Miriam, may G-d avenge her blood. But I would like to show all of you a side of Miriam, which even those who had her as a teacher may not have been aware of. I want to show you the side of her relationship with *Hashem*, through her prayers. Please let me read to you a poem she wrote that was found in the beginning of her siddur."

There was silence in the hall as the *Rav* read in his precise, gentle voice:

The Sounds of Prayer
(Translated from Hebrew by Shifra Shomron)

As the sounds of prayer rose, holy and pure,
I felt you, G-d.
For this quiet I longed
And the silence I calmed.
That which hurts the soul,
And dulls the longing.

My G-d,
Hear my pleading,
And remove the barriers from my soul.
Help me to pour the prayer
On a world of material and doing,
And also when suffering arrives,
To feel your love, G-d.

The *Rav* continued his speech, "Miriam was a wonderful person and a dedicated teacher. How often would I see her during the summer vacation busily xeroxing papers and getting ready for the next school year! And how many times would she give a student who hadn't liked the lunch here, her own food or extra food that she had brought with her for just such an occasion.

Miriam was a gentle person, a truly kind person. Her many students will bear witness to her special personality, and so will the soldiers who happily ate her rich cakes on *Shabbat* afternoons, sipped her warm soups on cold winter nights and answered her cheery hellos in the mornings. Her husband will bear witness to this. So will her children.

We have lost a dedicated teacher, a kind friend, a good wife and a good mother. May her blood be avenged and may we be comforted with the mourners of Zion."

The *Rav* finished his speech. No one clapped; it didn't seem right on this occasion…

A girl from the tenth grade got up and read a poem. Then another girl read a poem. Then a representative of the teachers got up and gave a long, painful speech. Several more girls read touching speeches.

And then an entire grade came to the front. Three girls had guitars. The grade sat down and, to the guitar accompaniment, sang slowly:

by Sivan Brown
[Translated from Hebrew by Shifra Shomron]

Arms that hug, a heart that is merciful and warm,
Lips that smile wide and don't speak words that harm.
So full of happiness and love, I
Ask: Miriam, how did you go
No reply.

Pain so strong that it can not be told,
Please just tell me that you're as happy there as of old.
An empty space from within that spreads wider still,
That no one else will ever manage to fill.

Chorus
Miriam, how did you go – suddenly one day,
I didn't even have time, my "good byes" to say.
And like from a dream I want to awake,
Miriam, just help me not to break.

Angel's tears, the sky is gray,
For you everyone is weeping today.
I will always love you and will never forget, so
The memories I'll take with me to everyplace I go.

The guitars strummed a few more sad notes, and then they started singing the song again from the beginning. This time, all the *Ulpana* joined in while wiping tears. "Arms that hug, a heart that is merciful and warm, lips that smile wide –" *Boom!* A huge explosion rocked the hall and all the windows rattled wildly.

Hysteria broke out, helped by the fact that the girls and staff were all in an emotional breakdown at the time. Efrat's first thought was, my G-d! That's a mortar! And she rose from her chair in shock. Girls around her were crying loudly, screaming, standing up or lying on the floor under the tables. Am I stupid? Efrat wondered. Why am I standing and exposing myself to shrapnel should another mortar fall? The thought only took seconds to register in her alert brain and she shakily sat back down on her chair, verifying that she wasn't hurt and that she was below window level.

She gazed around. The teachers were calming girls down, handing out cups of water and making sure no one was hurt.

Efrat seemed to be the only one not sobbing. She was still a bit shocked.

The community loudspeakers crackled and they heard an announcement to get into protected areas.

We aren't in a protected area, Efrat thought. Look at all those windows! And the ceiling isn't cement either!

They heard some jeeps pull up close to the *Ulpana* hall. Efrat recognized the Rav Shatz who walked in to the hall along with ambulance driver and several soldiers. After finding out that everyone was, thank G-d, O.K. (if a bit hysterical) the Rav Shatz ordered them to run in pairs to the *Ulpana* bomb shelter. "Quickly now!"

he ordered in his crisp, authoritative voice, and started talking to the *Rav*.

Efrat walked quickly from the hall to the bomb shelter. It was a gorgeous day; clear and sunny. She saw soldiers milling around a hole in the grass at the edge of the *Ulpana* grounds. So that's where the mortar fell, she realized.

In the bomb shelter, she found the girls divided into groups, chatting. They seemed to have calmed down a lot and only a few were still sobbing. The *Ulpana* psychologists walked around, offering juice and cookies and checking how the girls were coping.

Efrat accepted a cup of juice and slowly drank it. She didn't say a word. She wanted to call her parents to tell them she was fine. They must have heard the mortar fall, and if they found out that it had fallen in the *Ulpana* grounds, they would be worried.

Soon the *Rav* entered the bomb shelter along with the Rav Shatz. The Rav Shatz said something about several more mortars having fallen nearby, and that no one was injured. "Stay inside the building during recess," he warned. "We're been warned that more mortars are going to fall today." And he left.

Several weeks later and the *Ulpana* started with the construction of a new hall that would be safe against mortars. The old hall would function as a *Beit midrash*.

The *Ulpana* engraved the *Shabbat* eve song "*Eshet Chayil*" in soft gray letters upon the large picture of Miriam. The picture was then hung in the entrance hall of the *Ulpana*.

Chapter 16

Two weeks into the month of Kislev (December) and the twelfth grade gathered one evening before dinner to discuss the upcoming *Chanukiah* contest.

"Quiet, everyone!" Yael called out. "O.K." She continued when it was reasonably silent. "Who has an idea?" And she took out a red marker and moved to stand next to the board.

"I've got an idea!" Sarit said excitedly. "Listen everyone, it's really cute: each candle is a dwarf – that's seven dwarves and we also have Snow White as a candle and the prince as a candle; that accounts for all nine *chanukiah* candles."

"No, no," said Ayelet. "Listen, each candle is a teacher and the *Shamash* is the *Rav*."

The girls laughed but no one looked too eager to do it.

Yael wrote the ideas on the board. "Does anyone else have an idea?" She demanded.

The girls were silent.

Finally Shosh spoke up, "Look, this is our last year at the *Ulpana* and we won't get another chance... Do we want our *chanukiah* to just be cute and funny or do want to express an idea?!"

Efrat nodded in approval. Yes, she thought. Good for Shosh. She put her finger precisely on the point that was troubling me.

"You want to express an idea?" Yael asked. "No problem. But suggest an idea!"

Again the class was silent.

Then Rachel spoke up. "I've got an idea. And it's a really neat idea," she walked to the front of the class excitedly. "But it'll be a lot of work."

The twelfth grade waited for her to continue.

"Listen, we take a lot of matches. Almost a thousand matches, and on each match we write the name of a Jew who's been killed during this second *Intifada.* Then we glue the matches to cardboard and build a three dimensional *chanukiah!*"

Shosh quickly stood up, her eyes twinkling excitedly. "And for the background we'll paint a sunset and write on it the poem Blessed is the Match by Hanna Senesh!"

Efrat looked around at the girls. It was obvious that everyone was in favor of Rachel's suggestion.

"Fine," Yael said loudly. "Does everyone agree to Rachel's suggestion? Everyone does? Good! Tuesday night, at seven, whoever can should come help make the *chanukiah.* Meeting adjourned!"

As the grade scattered in groups, Merav and Efrat made their way to the biology lab.

"Let's get this over with," Merav sighed.

"I'll type up the first page, and you do the second," Efrat suggested.

"Fine." They each sat down next to a computer and entered the Word program.

"Let's see…" Efrat mused out loud. "Let's use Arial print size 12. And size 14 bold for a title."

Merav nodded, her silky black braid twitching against her light pink sweater.

They finished typing up their corrected report and printed it off. Efrat turned the biology lab lights off and Merav locked the door behind them. They headed down the steps and to the teachers' lounge. They placed the keys and the report in their biology teacher's drawer.

"Finished," Efrat said and smiled tiredly.

"Finally," Merav agreed. "If I had to type $C_6H_{12}O_6$ one more time I would have really blown up!"

Efrat laughed. "Come on, doing the graphs in Excel was much worse!"

"Yeah," Merav groaned at the memory. "It took us so long to get those right."

"Are you going to come Tuesday evening to help make the *chanukiah* for the contest?"

Merav shrugged regretfully. "I can't. I've got a driving lesson."

"Ah. Good luck!"

"Thanks," Merav laughed. "I really do need some good luck during my driving lessons."

~~~

Yair came home for Chanukah vacation.

"So, Effie, when do you get off?"

"Wednesday morning. After the *chanukiah* contest and the Rav's speech."

"Ha!" Yair grinned, "I got off before you..."

Efrat ignored him. She continued reading her book.

Yair chuckled and went with Yoram to go check the mail. When they came back with the mail, Efrat was still reading her book.

"Hey, Effie, give it a rest." Yoram's green eyes twinkled down at her. "*Ima* says that dinner is ready and that you're to come eat."

Efrat sighed, but dutifully placed her book on her desk and followed Yoram to the kitchen.

"What is the matter, Efrat?" Miri asked, concerned, as Efrat entered the kitchen.

Efrat shrugged and ran a gentle hand through her wavy brown hair. "I don't know, I'm just tired." And she really was tired, she realized. Tired of that odd feeling she'd had for the past couple months; a feeling that she and all of Israel were waiting for something. Something was going to happen. She knew it – she felt it. She was just tired of waiting for it.

Efrat poured some mushroom sauce on the potato borekas on her plate.

The phone rang loudly.

"Hello?" Miri answered. "Just a second," she covered the mouthpiece, "Efrat – it's for you."

Efrat walked over to the phone. "Hi?"

"Hello, this is Yael. Listen, we've decided to start making the *chanukiah* tonight. Can you come help?"

"Oh! Sure, I'll be at the *Ulpana* in half an hour."

"Great! Bye."

Efrat returned to the table. "I need to go down to the *Ulpana* soon."

"How come?" Miri asked. "Another biology report?"

Efrat smiled. "No, thank goodness. We're going to start making our *chanukiah* for the *Ulpana's chanukiah* contest. Every year each grade makes a *chanukiah* and the teachers judge them. The winning grade gets a prize."

"Ah," Miri smiled. "Sounds like fun."

Efrat didn't think that the word 'fun' quite described building a *chanukiah* out of the names of the fallen. And later that evening, at the *Ulpana*, she still hadn't changed her mind.

Yael and Reut had printed off a list of all the Jews killed in this second *Intifada*. Liat and Roni had brought about twenty boxes of matches from the cafeteria. Rachel was busy drawing out the shape of the *chanukiah* on stiff cardboard, and Efrat and Shosh were sitting at a desk carefully writing the names of the fallen on the matches with 0.4 pens. They had put some music on to make their work more pleasant.

"Oh, finally!" Rachel sat up and laid her pencil down. She picked up a large scissors and started cutting the cardboard.

"These lists don't end," Shosh groaned.

"I don't even recognize half of these names," Efrat said quietly. "Ah yes! I remember this fellow – on Tu B'Shvat, which had landed on a *Shabbat*, Arabs went to the hilltop that he lived on and knocked on the door. It was night time so he was suspicious and didn't open it. But the Arabs shot through the door, and he was killed and his wife and children saw it all, helpless. Terrible."

Yael and Roni joined them at the desk. Shosh got up and took a folded piece of paper out of her skirt pocket. "I copied Hanna Senesh's poem: Blessed is the Match," she said.

"Good," Rachel commented. "But we can't write it until we've painted the sunset background. And the paint will have to dry first."

"Fine," Shosh nodded, and put the paper back in her pocket. "I'll start painting the sunset background right now."

"Put a lot of red in it," Rachel suggested.

"Yes, that's what I thought," Shosh agreed. She started taking out the red, yellow and orange paints from a cardboard box in the corner of the classroom.

Efrat left Yael and Roni to microscopically continue writing the names of the fallen on the matches, and sat down by Shosh to watch her paint.

First the yellow, and stroke by stroke, brush by brush the stiff white paper became bright with light. Then came the turn of the orange paint – broad streams of orange which turned the light to flames. And then the red. Red to turn a fire into a sunset. Red to show the blood of the sinking sun, the sun that was murdered during the bright noon and whose blood now pours out into the evening sky until all the light is blotted out. And only darkness remains.

Shosh stopped painting and recited in a clear and soft voice:

> *Blessed is the match consumed*
> *In kindling flame.*
> *Blessed is the flame that burns*
> *In the secret fastness of the heart.*
> *Blessed is the heart with strength to stop*
> *Its beating for honor's sake.*
> *Blessed is the match consumed*
> *In kindling flame.*

[Hanna Senesh, May 2, 1944. Translated from the Hebrew by Marie Syrkin. From: Hanna Senesh Her Life and Diaries, page 253.]

Part III
In The Shadow
Of Disengagement

Chapter 17

"Ah," Efrat sighed happily, as she sat at the kitchen table after dinner and watched the colorful *chanukiah* candles slowly melt into warm colorful puddles of wax.

Yair looked at her and grinned.

Yoram, relaxing in the beige colored reclining chair, flipped a page of the newspaper he was glancing through. He folded the newspaper in half so that only the article he was reading was visible, loosened the red shoelaces of his brown boots, and continued reading.

A peaceful, drowsy atmosphere settled in the kitchen and in the living room.

Miri was sitting on the couch, crocheting a new *kippa* for Yair – she was making a blue and grey triangular pattern as a border for the white *kippa*.

Yair laughed, "It's too quiet here! At *Yeshiva*, there's always lots of noise."

"Quiet," Efrat hushed him gently. "Let's enjoy the quiet." She gazed intently at the flickering candle flames, her brown eyes mirroring the dancing bright lights of the *chanukiah* candles.

"Two blue, one gray," Miri counted out loud. "Yair has a point, Efrat. Let's talk about Chanukah."

"Hmm, Chanukah," Efrat sighed. "What holiday equals it? If it weren't for Chanukah, who knows if there would be a Jewish nation today?"

"Go on," Yair said, interested.

"Well," Efrat continued, speaking softly and still staring into the flames. "The Greeks were the rulers of Judea. In fact, they ruled a huge empire. And they introduced many things to Judea: athletics, horse races, idols, temples, literature… The Greek language was the international language. The Greek culture was charming, fascinating and cosmopolitan; the entire world was eager to learn and copy it! And…Judea was no exception," Efrat shook her pretty head sorrowfully. The entire family waited for her to continue; Yoram had laid aside his newspaper, Miri's crocheting was lying in her lap and Yair was cupping his chin in the palm of his hand, listening very intently to the story of Chanukah.

Efrat continued, talking to the flames which danced merrily in return. "The people of Judea were caught in the Hellenistic snare, and they too wanted to be modern, progressive and assimilated. In only a few decades, the Jewish society became very like the gentile society. Jerusalem the capital, Jerusalem the Holy City became no different from Athens, Tzidon or Acre. Jerusalem sank into the quagmire of idol worship and business – and sank deep. The social elite were in the lead; the High Priests, the government, the courts…and the masses followed their lead eagerly."

"So what happened?" Yair interrupted. "If the entire Jewish nation was in favor of becoming Hellenists, then how come there was a Hashmonian revolt?"

"Yair," Yoram explained, "not all that glitters is gold. Many Jews who were attracted at first to the glitter, realized in time that their own Jewish culture, traditions, religion and beliefs were (and are) far more precious; because they are true."

Yoram paused in his explanation and Efrat continued. "Only in the Jewish fringes were there a few stubborn Jews, extremely nationalistic and 'uncultured,' who refused to join the social-religious process of the Hellenistic progress. These Jews kept on observing G-d's commandments, and struggled fiercely against the High Priests and the government.

"Well, the Hellenistic Jews sought to stop this and as quickly as possible. Therefore they invited Antiochus Epiphanies to downtrod the 'progress refusers.' Antiochus acted according to the Hellenistic Jews' advice; his new laws forced sacrificing pigs to the Greek gods in the Temple in Jerusalem and in every city and village in Judea. His laws also forbid observing *Brit mila*, keeping the *Shabbat*, learning Torah and eating Kosher. Whoever transgressed a law was killed. And quite a few Jews were killed."

"So what did an observant Jew do?" Yair asked.

"Simple, he fled to the hills," Efrat answered. "He escaped

from the settled areas to the rugged hills of Judea and Samaria, to the edges of the Galilee. Away from the spying eyes and traitorous tongues of their Hellenistic brothers."

"Grievous!" Yair exclaimed. "Who can live like that, how come it took so long for the religious Jews to rebel?"

"People need a leader," Miri said thoughtfully. "The idea of rebelling against the Greek empire was an incredible idea. All the odds were against it succeeding. Do you think they would dare do that without a strong leader to follow?"

"One day they got their leader," Efrat continued. "An old man named Matityahu from the High Priest family was ordered by the Greeks to sacrifice a pig. He refused to do so! When a Hellenistic Jew stepped forward to do so instead of him, Matityahu killed the man and the pig. Then he escaped with his five sons to the hills. Slowly, slowly, people joined them. G-d was with them and after many hard fought battles, they managed to wrest Judean sovereignty from the Greek empire, and eradicate the majority of Hellenistic Jews.

"They decreed the holiday of Chanukah – an eight day holiday commemorating their dedication of the Holy Temple."

"Wow," Yair exclaimed. "I wonder, if I'd have lived then, would I have had the courage to join the Maccabees against the Greeks and the Hellenists? I mean, a bunch of farmers and shepherds fighting against numerous well trained and well armed Greek legions!"

Efrat turned away from the *chanukiahs* and looked Yair squarely in the eye, "The fact that Jews did join Matityahu and his sons, is one of the major miracles of Chanukah."

Yair nodded thoughtfully. Efrat turned back to watch the melting candles and Miri resumed her crocheting. Yoram returned to the article he had been reading.

Efrat stared at the yellow candle. It had melted down completely. Only a tiny flame remained. Impatiently, Efrat turned towards Yoram. Why did she have a feeling that she was waiting for something? It was a most unpleasant feeling! Something bad is going to happen soon, she thought. I wish I knew what it was; better to know what the difficulty is so that you can face it. Not knowing and waiting... is dreadful!

She glanced around. Everyone else seemed relaxed and

peaceful.

Yoram suddenly cleared his throat. The family turned towards him. "This is a very, um, interesting article I've just read. Listen: 'In a speech Prime Minister Ariel Sharon gave at the Herzliya Conference, Sharon announced that he intends, if he doesn't find an Arab partner, to unilaterally withdraw from the Gaza Strip and from part of the Northern Shomron. This will involve evacuating settlements. This Disengagement Plan is an exact opposite to things he had said only a year ago, such as *The verdict of Nitzarim is like the verdict of Tel Aviv.*'"

Yoram stopped reading. The room was very still.

Efrat smiled wryly. So that's the bad news I was waiting for, she thought to herself.

Yair said, trying to joke, but with a strange glint in his eyes, "Time for a second revolution. Hellenism is taking over again."

"Hmm," Miri said very quietly, "Perhaps the word 'revolution' is too strong. But a struggle there definitely will be."

"You bet there'll be a struggle!" Yair said hotly. "Our own Jewish Prime Minister wants to throw us from our homes! Do you think the people of Gush Katif will just pack their bags?!"

"Oh, no. We Gush Katifnics have our faults, but being hasty is not one of them. No one will even consider packing."

Yoram looked at his wife curiously, "Miri, what do you think is going to happen?"

"I think the Yesha Council will organize some big demonstrations, but only if we see that Sharon is really set on his – how did he call it? – Disengagement Plan, will there be a real struggle against this horrendous plan."

Yoram thought for a bit. "I do believe you're right," he said at last. "A few peaceful demonstrations, routine will continue as usual here in the Gush, and only if things look really serious will we start thinking about how to prevent this crazy plan."

Efrat rose from her chair in one swift move. "The candles have all burned out. I'm going to bed," she announced flatly and left the room. Soon afterwards, the other members of the Yefet family went to bed too.

Shifra Shomron

"I am Hashem, your G-d, who elevated you from the land of Egypt, open wide your mouth and I will fill it. But My people did not heed My voice and Israel did not desire me. So I let them follow their heart's fantasies, they follow their own counsels. If only My people would heed Me, if Israel would walk in My ways. In an instant I would subdue their foes, and against their tormentors turn My hand." (From the Shachrit morning prayer service.)

Chapter 18

It was the last night of Chanukah. The Yefets had invited the Eisleys over for dinner.

"Come in, come in," Miri greeted them warmly.

"Brrr, it's cold outside," Mrs. Eisley shivered. "Oh, it's nice and warm in here."

Yoram nodded, "That's because we have both radiators on."

Mr. and Mrs. Eisley took their coats off and sat down at the table. Yoram and Miri joined them.

"So, back to work tomorrow?" Mr. Eisley teased Yoram.

"What do you mean back to work," Yoram protested, grinning. "You know a vegetable inspector never has a vacation!"

"What are you checking this season?"

"Five dunam of green onion and seven dunam of lettuce."

"Nice," Mr. Eisley nodded.

Miri finished setting the table with refreshments, and poured them all a hot cup of tea.

"So," Mrs. Eisley started after a short pause of steady munching. "What do you think of 'Crime' Minister's Sharon crazy plan?"

"You mean this 'Disengagement Plan'?" Miri asked, exchanging a look with her husband.

"That's the one," Mrs. Eisley snorted. "Mind you, my husband here doesn't think it'll happen but –"

" 'Course it won't," Mr. Eisley put in. "Bunch of bunk, made up just to get the courts and the media distracted from all his illegal affairs, you know, the Greek Island affair… Clever man, Sharon. Knows how left wing the courts and the media are. Well, now they'll all chew their cuds over this new plan, and forget about his crimes." Mr. Eisley helped himself to another latke.

"So you don't think Sharon is serious?" Yoram asked, surprised.

"Of course not!" Mr. Eisley answered staunchly, not bothered at all by Yoram's not agreeing with him. "Heck, they've been trying to get us out of here since Oslo back in 1993. They didn't succeed then and they won't succeed now either. It's just a scheme to divert the media and the courts' attention."

"Well, I don't know how it'll develop," Mrs. Eisley put in angrily. "I think it's still too early to tell. But it makes me mad, it does; that a Jewish Prime Minister can even contemplate throwing Jews from their homes! Shame on him!"

"I am sure that Gush Katif and all the Jews in Israel who care about our G-d-given land will do all they can to prevent this expulsion plan," Miri said hopefully. "After all, both Labor and Likud governments have encouraged us throughout the years to settle this area. Gush Katif isn't an outpost; we're twenty-one thriving communities, thousands of families... if they throw us from our homes, no place in Israel is safe!"

Mrs. Eisley shook her round face solemnly. "Miri, my dear," she said slowly, "you have no idea how little the average Israeli knows or cares about Gush Katif. For all they know, we're fifteen caravans in the middle of the desert with camels on our front lawns."

They all laughed at this bizarre idea.

"I'm not kidding!" Mrs. Eisley said sternly though her blue eyes twinkled. "For years all they've heard in the news about Gush Katif is how many mortars fall here each day and how many soldiers are killed in the area." She paused to take another sip from her tea, "Did you see the news this morning?" She asked.

"No," Yoram and Miri shook their heads.

"Well, I did," she said shortly. "And all they did was talk about this 'Disengagement plan'. And in order to give their viewers an idea of how Gush Katif looks they showed them –"

"An aerial picture of the Gush?" Miri interrupted.

Mrs. Eisley looked at her, shocked. "Are you kidding? Our left wing media doesn't want the public to know how big and developed Gush Katif really is – why, then the public might protest, and not want Sharon to give it away!"

Miri nodded in agreement.

"So what did they show?" Yoram asked curiously.

"They showed an army jeep driving between the Kissufim and Gefen junctions," Mrs. Eisley paused.

"But that's not even in the Gush!" Miri said, outraged.

"Tell that to them," Mrs. Eisley shrugged. "They know that, but they have their own agenda. However they also took a picture from the top of the hill – right before Gadid. Now, from that location you see the entire community of Neve Dekalim spread out before you."

"Right," Miri and Yoram agreed.

"But they made sure to take a picture only of one row of houses, and they must have lied down to take it, since three quarters of the T.V. screen showed only sand and then at the top of the screen was one row of houses."

"So now everyone in Israel thinks that Gush Katif is about ten houses and one street with a jeep," Yoram said dryly.

"What we need to do," Miri said earnestly, "is to go door to door and reach as many people as we can, and sit down with them and explain to them what Gush Katif really is. Give speeches, hand out flyers... that sort of thing. We must raise national awareness, and increase the nation's knowledge."

"I agree," Mrs. Eisley said.

"Agree to what?" Yair asked, as he and Efrat burst into the house.

"Where were you?" Miri asked. "I told you two to be home on time for dinner."

Yair shrugged, "I was at the other end of town playing basketball with some friends. I was about to head home, when some mortars fell, so I was stuck at the Cohens for the past half hour."

Efrat laughed. "I didn't even hear any mortars! Lipaz and I were reviewing a couple of chapters in the book of Melachim 1, and we only just finished. It's important," she groaned, "tomorrow we have a huge test on it."

"Why don't you two sit down," Yoram suggested. "Have some latkes, before I finish them off," he added, his green eyes dancing merrily.

Efrat and Yair sat down and put some latkes on their plates.

The room was silent.

"Well, don't let us bother your conversation," Yair said politely.

"How's *Yeshiva?*" Mr. Eisley asked him.

"Fine," Yair answered.

"Do you and your friends discuss the Disengagement Plan?" Mrs. Eisley asked Yair.

"Discuss what?"

"Discuss 'Crime' Minister Sharon's idea of throwing us from our homes," Mrs. Eisley explained.

"Oh, that," Yair shrugged. "We haven't talked about it much, but a lot of my friends don't think it'll happen."

Mr. Eisley nodded approvingly, "Smart kids."

"Look, whether we think it'll happen or not, we'll all join the struggle to prevent the expulsion plan. We're just waiting for the struggle to start," Yair explained.

Mrs. Eisley looked pleased. "Excellent, with the youth impatient, the struggle will start soon."

"It'll have to," Yoram said grimly. "Because from what you said earlier this evening, it sounds like the media is already up in arms against us and egging Disengagement on."

Rufus plodded into the room, and Efrat pet him gently. It was obvious, she thought, that Mr. Eisley didn't think the expulsion would happen. Mrs. Eisley, however, was really worked up over the very idea of expulsion. And what about her own family? She wondered. *Aba* seemed to think that it could very possibly happen. *Ima*, she hesitated and then chuckled, it would be like *Ima* to go door to door trying to convince people that this was a very bad idea of the Prime Minister. And Yair? She looked carefully at Yair's handsome face, determined jaw, the glint in his eyes... Yair, she thought, will not hesitate to act according to what he deems is right, no matter the personal cost. And while this last thought troubled her, it also made her proud.

Chapter 19

That night it poured. Hard sheets of rain washed the red roofs clean, streamed through the black streets and soaked through the golden sand dunes. Thunder roared dully and lightening tore the dark night sky illuminating the heavy gray clouds, and flashing briefly upon the falling rain drops.

"Come on," Efrat whispered as she lay in bed listening to the loud patter of the falling rain. "Keep on pouring! Wash the country – make it clean. Drench the land – make the plants grow. Fill the Kinneret – make the Sea of Galilee rise."

Thunder rumbled in the distance. The rain kept on falling heavily. Efrat smiled contently, and pulled her soft comforter up to her chin.

A bit later and the new moon managed to free itself from behind a large gray cloud. Happily sailing through the turbulent sky, the cold light of the sliver of a moon penetrated the drawn blinds of Efrat's room. She was fast asleep.

The next morning as Efrat walked down to the *Ulpana*, she breathed deeply. The morning air was cool and fresh after the storm of the past night. The sky was a light gray, but purple storm clouds heavy with rain still hovered threateningly on the horizon over the calm Mediterranean Sea. Efrat's brown eyes glinted with suppressed joy. Neve Dekalim was beautiful in all weather, but especially on a fresh crisp winter morning after one storm had passed and the other still on its way.

The storm broke only after Efrat returned home from the *Ulpana*; she'd just closed the front door behind her when drops started falling from the purple mass above – drops that soon quickened into a heavy patter.

"Oh, good!" Miri exclaimed. "You're home just in time. I was afraid that you would get caught in the rain."

"Missed it," Efrat said almost regrettably.

The front door slammed and Yair entered the house. "Look at me," he demanded. "Only five minutes in this rain and I am drenched!"

Efrat laughed. "As long as it doesn't make you grow any taller…"

Yair snorted, his eyes twinkling merrily.

"Yair, go change into dry clothing, and then come here and tell us why you are home," Miri ordered her son.

A short time later, when Yair had changed into dry clothing and was sitting at the kitchen table drinking some hot chocolate, he started explaining. "Well, it's like this: nearly all my class went to Ashkelon just now to try to convince people to vote against Sharon's Disengagement Plan should it come to a national referendum."

"What an excellent idea," Miri said excitedly. "And why didn't you go too?" She demanded.

"Really, *Ima*! Just look at this weather," Yair pointed at the large window down which the rain was sliding non-stop. The trees could be seen leaning from the force of the wind, and some bright lightening flickered in the distance.

Efrat shivered, "Brrr, your classmates are actually going door to door in this weather?!"

Yair nodded, "My thoughts exactly. Anyhow," he demanded of his mother, "why is it such an 'excellent idea'? We don't know that there will be a national referendum. And if there isn't a national referendum all the hard work just goes to waste!"

Miri looked at her son earnestly. "First of all, if there is a national referendum then it's good that we start convincing people as soon as possible to vote against Disengagement. Secondly, it's always good to talk to people, to our Jewish nation, and remind them that this land is ours, given to us by G-d and that we need to fight the Arabs – not throw the Jews out. We need as many people converted to our way of thinking as possible. The more people who know the truth, the more people applying pressure against this expulsion plan via demonstrations and, perhaps, a referendum in the future."

Yair nodded. "O.K. I agree. But in this weather?!"

"It really isn't the nicest weather in which to be going door to door, is it?" Miri agreed. She looked out the window, musing. Suddenly she smiled brightly. "Tomorrow the weather is supposed to be clear to partly cloudy, no rain in the forecast. I say you two stay home from school, Yoram will stay home from work and we will all go door to door!"

Yair shrugged. "Pick a city," he said dryly.

"*Ima*, do I have to miss school?" Efrat complained. "I'll be missing two hours of biology and two hours of math and one hour of Bible —"

"Efrat," Miri said gently. "This time, the first time, I would really like us all to go. In the future it will be up to you; maybe you'll go with friends once a week."

At that Efrat chuckled. "If Yair's grade went today, then you can bet that *Ulpana* girls will start going too. We don't like it when the Katif Yeshiva gets ahead of us!"

"Good, then it is settled. You two might want to spend the evening preparing yourselves – how you'll introduce yourselves, what you will say, which points you want to stress…"

Yair gulped. "Sheesh!" He turned to Efrat and grinned, "Hey Effie, you'll do all the talking, right?"

Efrat shook her head.

"Oh, come on, please! Please!"

"No way. We'll both talk."

Yair sighed. "Fine, be mean. Now I need to concentrate on what I'll say."

"Good idea," Miri commented. "Start listing the different aspects."

"Huh?"

"Write down all the arguments not to give Gush Katif to the Arabs," Efrat explained quickly. "Oh, here, I'll do it," she said impatiently.

"No, not in here please. I want to start getting dinner ready," Miri commented.

"Fine, we'll do it at my desk."

Efrat seated herself at her desk, and turned the desk lamp on. Yair also sat down and silently handed her a large sheet of paper and a black pen.

"Well, number one…" Efrat hesitated.

"'Cause we don't give our land to our enemy," Yair said swiftly. "Especially when they are bombing us and shooting us…"

"Oh, that's good." Efrat nodded and wrote it down, saying as she did so, "That is simple enough and true enough that everyone ought to agree with that."

Yair snorted. "Don't be so naïve. You know how many left wingers there are in Israel!"

"Well, that's why we have to have lots of reasons, not just one. O.K. number two – because G-d gave us this land. Number three – because Jews have lived here in the Gaza Strip since the Second Temple period until the 1929 riots when the British kicked them out. Number four, your turn Yair…" And they kept at it through-out the evening. They also took turns at one of them playing the person to be convinced and the other one trying to convince them.

"Dinner!" Miri called loudly.

"Come on, Yair, I'm hungry."

"Wait, did we list the economic reasons?"

Efrat checked the list. "Yes, that was reason number five."

"What about the security reasons?"

"Reason number four."

"And the –"

"Stop it Yair! I'm not writing down any more reasons."

"I'm worried. What if they out talk us? What if we don't manage to convince them?"

Efrat chuckled. "Once we start talking we'll be fine. It's the first ten minutes that I'm worried about."

"Hey, Effie, we'll stick together – right? I'm not going to a house by myself."

"Don't fear. Of course we'll stay a pair! Hey *Ima*, Yair and I want to stay together tomorrow," Efrat said to her mother as they walked into the kitchen.

Miri smiled. "Of course. *Aba* and I will be one pair, and you and Yair will be another. Perhaps I can talk the Eisleys into joining us."

The next day dawned bright and early. As they all dressed a bit more carefully than usual, each Yefet family member tried to calm himself.

"I've gone over all the arguments about one hundred times. And I believe and agree with each one. I'm more prepared for this than I've been for any test," Yair thought as he tied his shoes.

"Two hours of biology! I can't believe I'm missing two hours of biology! And with our report due next Tuesday!" Efrat stopped brushing her long wavy brown hair. "But it's for a good cause," she said out loud, speaking earnestly to the pretty reflection in her mirror. Suddenly Efrat gave a brittle laugh, "a good cause?! It's to save our homes, our land, our nation!" And she finished brushing her hair with fast furious strokes.

"I hope Efrat and Yair won't be too shy to speak," Miri thought anxiously. "I know how Yair is when it comes to speaking with strangers…" She smoothed the bed sheet carefully, and took comfort in its perfect flatness. "Oh, with Hashem's help they'll be fine," she reassured herself. "And it's a wonderful learning experience too!" She grinned mockingly to herself.

"How on earth did Miri manage to convince me into going?" Yoram groaned as he neatly tucked his green checkered shirt into his brown pants. "I need to supervise the lettuce cutting today! Instead, I had to leave Dvir in charge. True, he's capable, but…" Yoram sighed. Miri's words echoed in his mind: "My dear, if we don't all do everything in our power to prevent Prime Minister Sharon's expulsion plan, then you won't have any hothouses left to check lettuce in!" Yoram shrugged helplessly. She was right, he knew. And now their family, and indeed all the Gush, was setting forth on a campaign to convince every Dan, Levy and Shimon to their right to the land.

~~~

"Right, well, call us on your cell-phone if you need us. Try not to stay too long with each family – the more people we reach, the better. Efrat, Yair – we'll meet back here in the parking lot in a few hours." Yoram smiled steadily, encouragingly, his green eyes serious. "Good luck!"

Efrat nodded excitedly. "You too, *Ima* and *Aba*. I mean, good luck to you also. Come on, Yair!"

Yair knocked hesitantly on the first door. They heard approaching footsteps and then the door opened.

"Good morning," an elderly man greeted them in a gruff tone.

Glancing at her brother, Efrat spoke first: "Good morning, sir. We are teenagers from Gush Katif, and –"

"We have come to explain the importance of keeping Gush Katif, our homes," Yair continued, rather bluntly.

A shadow of a smile flickered over the elderly man's lips. Politely he held the door open for them. "Come in, come in, make yourselves comfortable."

They sat down on the couch, their host in the armchair opposite them. The room was quiet. Light green striped curtains kept the room in a comfortably dimmed light.

Surprisingly, Yair took the initiative. "Perhaps, Sir –"

"My name is Rafule. Rafule Levran," their host put in.

"Well, Mr. Levran, perhaps it would be best if you let us know where you stand on this 'Disengagement' issue."

Efrat glanced at her brother with some surprise. That was a really good idea.

Their host studied them for a few seconds. Then, rising to his feet, he brought over a blank sheet of paper and a pen.

"Easier to draw," he explained gruffly. He started drawing:

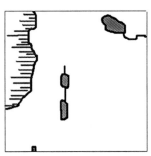

"This rough map," he said, *"shows the borders of the land the Almighty promised to us."*

He continued drawing another map:

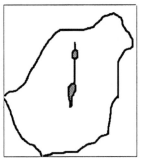

"This is the kingdom of David and Shlomo."

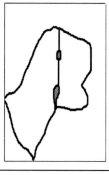

"This is the land conquered by Yehoshua and the tribes of Israel."

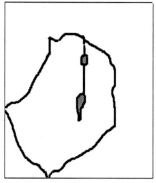

"In the times of the Hasmonian Kings."

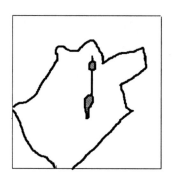

"According to the British Mandate."

"According to the U.N."

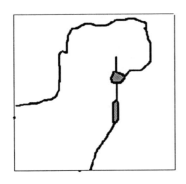

"After the
Six-Day War."

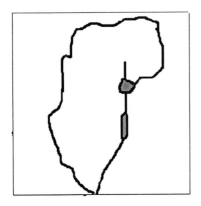

"Today"

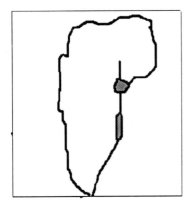

"Sharon's
Withdrawal Plan"

"And," he paused and looked at them through warm brown eyes under bristling eyebrows. "I have absolutely no desire to see the state look like this (he drew it quickly) according to Sharon's withdrawal plan."

"Grievous!" Yair said leaning over to look. "Can you imagine what the map of Israel would look like without Gaza, without Gush Katif?!"

"And it most probably would not end there," Mr. Levran pointed out.

"Right," Efrat agreed. "If," she faltered. "If Gush Katif is given away, what is to stop the government from giving away more and more Jewish communities until eventually all Judea and Samaria have been given away too?!"

The old man nodded. "Right." He smiled, "You know, I remember back in 1967 when we liberated Gaza."

"During the Six Day war," Yair put in.

"Exactly. And our commander was so excited. You see, his family had lived there for generations until 1929."

"Ah, the 1929 Arab riots," Efrat said slowly.

"I'm glad you two know your Jewish history," Mr. Levran said approvingly. "So few young people do these days," he sighed.

"Please continue," Yair put in, "you stopped in the middle – all I know about the 1929 Arab riots is that 67 Jews were massacred in Hevron. And the British wouldn't let the Jews return to their homes afterwards."

"Well," Mr. Levran continued, "the riots in Hevron are the most infamous, but in Tsfat, 18 Jews were massacred (though the survivors returned to their homes afterwards). And in Gaza, the Jews defended themselves against the beastly Arab mobs. But the British banished the Jews from Gaza and wouldn't let them return to the Jewish community in Gaza that had existed nonstop since the Second Temple period."

"And then we Jews reconquered it in 1967 and resettled it in the 1970s," Efrat concluded, smiling proudly.

"And now in the twenty first century our own Jewish government wants to give it to the Arabs!" Yair continued hotly.

"It's bad, it's very bad," Mr. Levran sighed. "Our government is willing to appease our enemy instead of fighting them. Give them Gush Katif for a short spell of quiet."

"'Short spell' is right," Efrat said angrily. "When the Arabs can fire mortars from our communities they'll reach the large coastal city Ashkelon!"

"And they will have all the weapons they need; they won't have to smuggle them in through tunnels from Egypt anymore. Our soldiers won't be able to prevent it in the slightest," Yair added.

"The situation does look hopeless," Mr. Levran agreed. "But," he continued and a new stern tone rang in his gruff voice, "I'm with you. And so are many others. But we're waiting for you guys, for the people of Gush Katif, to act. I'm on your side; call a demonstration and I'll be there. I'm 86 years old and have seen my share of fighting, but I'm willing to be arrested for the cause of a greater Israel, a proud, strong, Jewish Israel." His voice rang out deep and strong. It vibrated through the small rather dim living room. "I fought against the British, I fought against the Arabs many times, and now it is the time for a struggle against the Jewish government." His face wrinkled into a bright smile. "I'm willing, and with youth like you two, we can win!"

Yair reached over and shook Mr. Levran's hand warmly. Efrat beamed, "Excellent!" she said.

Yair glanced at his watch. "Mr. Levran, thank you very much for your time. We've had a great conversation! But Efrat and I want to meet as many families as we can today..."

"Sure!" Mr. Levran smiled, a bit sadly. "Hey, if you're ever in this neighborhood again, stop by. I insist!"

Efrat smiled warmly, "sure, Mr. Levran. And if you come to the Gush, well, we live in Neve Dekalim. Ask for the Yefet family. Here is our phone number. We'd love to show you around – the Gush is our home!"

Mr. Levran escorted them to the door.

Efrat knocked on the next door. No answer. She knocked again. Still no answer.

"Come on, Effie. Guess no one is home. Let's try the next house," Yair said. Efrat agreed and they moved on.

Meanwhile, Miri and Yoram were having a more difficult time.

"Really, Shuli," Yoram protested, "you have no problem with Jewish men, women, and children being thrown from their homes by Jewish soldiers?!"

"I would, of course, prefer the police do that part," the blonde haired woman sitting stiffly opposite Miri and Yoram said coldly. "After all, my son is in the army and I don't want him to have any bad dreams..." She shuddered and sniffed.

"Do you realize that throwing Jews from their homes is just like what the Gentiles have been doing to us for 2,000 years of exile. They expelled us from Spain, France, England, Poland, Russia... and now Israel, the Jewish State, will behave like those anti-Jewish gentiles!" Miri said, trying to stay calm.

"But my dear," the blonde woman said calmly and very slowly as if speaking to a thick-headed child. "It will bring peace!"

"Why will it bring peace?" Yoram asked.

The woman looked surprised. "Um, because, well, because we'll have given them their land back. What they have been asking for!"

"Then perhaps you can explain to me why the Arabs fought us in 1967 – before we had Gaza." Yoram spoke politely.

"Well," the blonde woman hesitated, clearly at a loss for words.

"And why they fought us in 1956."

"Um, well, um..."

"And in 1948."

"And the 1936 – 1939 Arab riots, and the 1929 Arab riots. And in 1921, and 1920, and Tel Chai..." Miri said smoothly. "We didn't, you know, even have a State back then!"

"Well, in any case," their hostess replied icily, "now they have promised that if we give them Gaza, they'll give us peace. It's an excellent deal and a few caravans that some crazy Jews live in won't stop us!"

Miri looked shocked. Yoram tried to hide a smile, his green eyes twinkling merrily. To tell the truth, he was rather enjoying himself now.

"Dear," Miri said, "do you really think that Gush Katif is merely a few caravans?"

"Of course," Shuli purred. "I saw the news a bit ago – one row of houses in vast empty sand dunes." She laughed, "tiny and insignificant."

Yoram sighed. "Ms, you see only what the media wants you to see. Let me show you a more accurate picture of Gush Katif." He handed her several colorful pamphlets full of pictures and information about the Gush.

Shuli picked one up. Pictures of happy children jumped up at her; large three story houses, two story houses, rambling one story houses stood over her; dunams of gray hothouses – their clear plastic rippling in the sea breeze and their interiors full of red tomatoes still on the vines, green onions tall and mysterious, cucumbers ready to be picked... spread before her like a rolling sea; but not just pictures – sentences pierced her painfully:

"The story of the settlers of Gush Katif is the story of pioneers that built their homes in the portion of the tribe of Yehuda – where Jewish settlements thrived until the 1929 Arab riots.

"In the early '70s, Jewish settlements were renewed in the Gaza strip with the encouragement of the Israeli governments who realized the moral and security importance of a Jewish hold in the area.

"Today Gush Katif boasts twenty one blooming communities, which are home to some 8,000 settlers, religious and non-religious,

Sabras and *Olim*.

"A desert of dunes has become the spearhead of Israeli agriculture in Israel and throughout the world. This is in addition to the many educational institutions and a growing industrial area.

"Since the eve of Rosh Hashanah, the residents of Gush Katif have bravely faced about 11,000 terror attacks and about 4,000 mortars and kassam rockets. Despite these hardships, more than 300 families have joined the ranks of Gush Katif."

[A Gush Katif pamphlet. Translated from the Hebrew by Shifra Shomron.]

Shuli stopped reading and stared at the picture of the sweet little girl holding a sign that read in clumsy childish handwriting: Neve Dekalim is my home, my father's and mother's home, and my Grandma's and Grandpa's home.

"As you can see," Miri said gently, breaking the silence she and Yoram had kept while the woman opposite them had perused one of the pamphlets, "Gush Katif is much, much more than 'a few caravans'."

Shuli nodded briefly. She felt as if fogs were being cleaned from her head. "Why?" She said, aghast. "Why didn't the media tell us the truth? Why did they let me and millions of other Jews believe in warped pictures and false statements?" And she started crying.

Yoram shifted uncomfortably in his chair.

"Why are you crying?" Miri asked softly.

"Because I am afraid," the woman sobbed. "I only have one child. And he is a soldier serving in Gaza, and soldiers are getting killed there all the time! I want him to be safe, and I thought that if we gave away Gush Katif, the Arabs would stop killing us!"

Yoram looked at her intensely. "No," he said. "If we give away Gush Katif, it will be a huge victory for the Arabs of K'han Yunis, of Dir El Balakh and of Rafiach! A huge victory for every Arab who has shot at us, fired bombs at us or tried to infiltrate our communities. They will have learned that they can attack Jews, and not only will the Jewish government not defend the Jews, but the Jewish government will eventually throw those Jews from their homes and give that land to the attacking Arabs! And, thus encouraged, many more Jews will be killed. I understand why you're scared. And I'm scared too. But our only chance is to put enough pressure on the Prime Minister that'll convince him that what he is planning is a deadly mistake and that he needs to defend the Jews instead."

Shuli had stopped weeping, and was hanging onto Yoram's every word. "Do you have some more pamphlets you can give me?" She asked. "I'd like to show them to my neighbors..."

Silently, Yoram took out several more from the bag he was carrying and handed them to her.

Miri took out a bag of fresh dill. "This was grown in hothouses in B'dolach. Don't worry, my husband checked it – it's bug-free," she added, though the woman she was handing them to didn't look as if she had ever known to check whether there were any insects in her vegetables.

"Bug-free?" She repeated curiously.

Yoram explained. "According to Jewish law, one is not allowed to eat insects. Gush Katif specializes in growing insect-free vegetables. All you need to do is rinse them before eating them."

Yoram and Miri got up to leave. Shuli followed them to the door. Before they left she said passionately, "Thank you, for taking the wool from my eyes!"

"Goodness!" Miri exclaimed to Yoram outside the house. "That was tough!"

Yoram agreed.

Chapter 20

The entire Gush jumped on the bandwagon of "Face to Face" – going door to door and talking to secular and religious, young and old, rich and poor. To everyone they gave pamphlets, a few vegetables grown in Gush Katif, and a CD showing beautiful pictures of lovely, endangered Gush Katif.

During recesses, free periods and late into the night, the *Ulpana* girls stood and prepared bags and bags each filled with a pamphlet, vegetables and a disc. They put music on to make the time pass more pleasantly and worked busily; their pretty faces youthful and cheery.

Did they believe Disengagement would happen? No, they did not. Certainly not at this stage when they were busy preparing bags and going Face to Face. With each person that they convinced that Gush Katif shouldn't be given to the Arabs, they felt more positive that a horrible Disengagement could never happen – so many people were on their side!

Such innocence is understandable and sweet in the young, but the awakening is rude. And not all awaken.

Efrat was shocked one morning in the month of Tevet (December) when she saw a teenager whom she knew wearing a bright orange Star of David pinned to her black coat.

"Ortal, why are you wearing that?!" Efrat asked, completely shocked.

"This?" Ortal pointed to the orange Star of David.

Efrat nodded, not managing to tear her eyes away from it.

Ortal explained, "It's our new campaign. Just as in World War Two, the point was to make the world *Judenrein* – free from Jews, we're showing that Prime Minister Sharon's Disengagement Plan is the same idea; to make the Gaza strip *Judenrein*."

Efrat thought it over for a second. Ortal's explanation was

good, but "I see, Ortal. But when I see that orange Star of David, I think immediately of the yellow Star of David and the Holocaust – killing Jews, mass murdering Jews. Prime Minister Sharon wants to expel, not kill us!"

Ortal argued back: "The point is to shock the people. Not everyone is convinced by pretty pictures, simple logic and tasty vegetables. Some people need graphic images, need to be shocked into realizing that throwing Jews from their homes was the first step in the Holocaust – *Judenrein*!" She spat the last word out as though it had a putrid taste.

"Well, I won't wear one!" Efrat declared. "I'd never forgive myself if it caused a Holocaust survivor to faint or something…"

Ortal agreed. "Yes, I'm a bit afraid of that aspect myself…" but her voice trailed off as they both saw old Mrs. Freitsky walking with her frail husband across the street. Mrs. Freitsky was beaming all over her round winkled face. Very visibly pinned on her dark felt cloak was a big orange Star of David.

Efrat shrugged helplessly. "Well," she grinned weakly, "I guess some Holocaust survivors agree with you."

And even after the huge outcry the media gave regarding the orange Star of David, the furious comments of certain people in high quarters, and the new law that was passed in Israel forbidding political uses of terms or symbols connected with the Holocaust – old Mrs. Freitsky still walked around town determinedly wearing an orange Star of David pinned to her clothes in clear view.

The Orange Star

By Reuven Koret, Publisher of Israel Insider
December 26, 2004 (www.israelinsider.com)

The six-pointed Magen David is perhaps the most enduring representation of Jewishness. It adorns the Israeli flag. It appears on every synagogue. It hangs around the neck of many a proud Jew. It is to Judaism what the cross is to Christianity or the crescent is to Muslims. It is the symbol of our nationhood, our peoplehood.

So when the residents of Gush Katif decided to create orange badges in that shape, and wear them, I wondered: what's the big deal? I am not being disingenuous here. The initiators of the campaign were suggesting an association with the yellow Shields of David that the Germans forced the Jews to wear to single them for discrimination, for deportation and, eventually, for destruction. The residents of Gaza and northern Samaria are indeed the objects of discrimination and deportation, their communities slated for destruction – except those parts which may be handed over, intact, to Israel's enemies.

No one is equating Sharon with Hitler, or the IDF and Israeli police with the German Nazis or their collaborators. No one is saying that the disengagement process will lead to Death Camps – although the reality is that the government is preparing mass detention camps, and the process it is driving with demonic fervor will almost certainly result in needless deaths. The conscientious objectors are making a statement that what the Sharon government has arrogated to do – expelling thousands of citizens and eliminating whole communities is an act unprecedented in a democracy, certainly in recent decades, and not an act that can or should be accepted quietly or with equanimity.

Settlers bow to pressure, halt orange star campaign

By Nir Hasson, December 24, 2004, Haaretz

Bowing to public pressure, the organizers of the orange Star of David initiative announced yesterday they would stop distributing the orange stars, but said they would not call on people to stop wearing them.

On Wednesday, the Yesha Council of Settlements and MK Effi Eitam, together with several public figures, called on people to stop wearing the badge.

"For the moment, the badge has made its point, which was to shock people into thinking how Holocaust survivors in Gush Katif must feel these days," said Ronny Bakshi, one of the initiative's organizers, who admitted that opposition to the badge was greater than anticipated. "The Yesha Council can't help but condemn the matter, and I understand them. However, I will continue wearing the badge." At any rate, the organizers of the initiative apologized to Holocaust survivors for their action. Earlier in the day, Israel Defense Forces Manpower Division chief Major General Elazar Stern said settlers who wear an orange Star of David are Holocaust deniers.

In an interview on Channel 2's "Meet the Press," Stern called the phenomenon "madness," and noted "it will make it difficult for me to prevent soldiers from gloating over their [the settlers'] misfortune." Stern added that "these are not our people. Settlers who wear an orange star are Holocaust deniers, because if what was done in the Holocaust resembles what we are doing to them, it means the Holocaust was not so terrible or unique. I spoke to my parents [both of whom are Holocaust survivors] about it," Stern said. "When I spoke to them about the orange star they used the word 'madness,'" he said. "Let it be clear to everyone that when they tell us to evacuate, we will evacuate, and no threats, no equation to anything will deter us from our job," Stern said.

And, in spite of everything, life continued as normal.

Motzei Shabbat, 28 Tevet, 5765 (January 9, 2005)

Dear Mem,

Shabbat was absolutely lovely! After the morning meal, as it was a bright sunny day, Yair and I went to go meet Aba, who had already left with Beauty to "the meadow." We went there the long way, since I had forgotten whether Aba had said he would be at the soccer field or at "the meadow." Since he wasn't at the soccer field, forward ho to "the meadow!"

Mem, it was lovely! The sun was warm, the sky blue, the wind delightfully refreshing and the sand firm beneath one's feet. We gaily walked past the big dune Kir HaMavet and reached "the meadow." We call that place "the meadow," because it is generally greener than any other area in the sand dunes, and one really felt as though one had reached a meadow – a secret oasis.

Anyhow, "the meadow" was all lush with winter weeds, and the air was poignant with the scent of eucalyptus – from the tree that was, sadly, lopped down.

Beauty came rushing to meet us! Aba had found two small turtles! Interestingly enough, there isn't a concept of capture / hunting regarding turtles in Jewish law; it is not forbidden on Shabbat, because they are so slow. Yair found an old rusty pail to put them in and we went home because Beauty was thirsty and tired.

So much has happened this week, but I don't even want to think about it all. Hashem manages things such that they have a way of working out.

Well, Yair has already practiced his clarinet tonight, and right now he is watching a very comical movie. I need to study a bit for a test in micro-organisms.

G'night,

Effie.

Chapter 21

The month of Shvat 5765 (January) dawned upon the world. Shvat, the month when the almond trees flower white and fresh. When trees, awake from their winter slumber, first start to bud and show the gray world new green leaves. Oh, Shvat! That precious month of rejuvenation, of new energy running from the blossoming trees, spreading through the earth and warming it and even soaring up human limbs; starting from the feet – steady upon the earth, and reaching the head.

Half the month passed, leaving the world that much prettier and merrier a place to be in. Then came the fifteenth of Shvat, Tu B'Shvat, the New Year for the trees. On Tu B'Shvat it is customary to plant trees, and do a special feast in which one eats dried fruit and one praises the fruit of The Land, and gives thanks to the Almighty for them.

Efrat, together with her classmates, planted vines along one of the sides of the basketball court the *Ulpana* had built recently in memory of their beloved sports teacher who had died of cancer the past summer.

Efrat finished patting down the sand around the small vine she had just planted. A spur winged plover trilled sharply overhead and glided gracefully to a rest on an acacia branch nearby. It cocked its head curiously at the teenage girls busy planting small vines or busy resting on the golden sand and chatting.

"Man is like the tree of the field," the sages have said, and indeed, Efrat thought, our roots go down deep in this land. All the deeper, perhaps, because it is sand dune land and ones roots need go deep down in order to reach the life restoring water. Efrat sighed; Disengagement was casting its ugly shadow over everything. Right now she had been wondering whether they would be in Gush Katif long enough to see these small frail vines grow to be big, spread out and cover the fencing that surrounded the new basketball court. And... she wasn't sure that they would.

Miri was still going 'door to door' every evening, and generally came home happy with the evenings' good work. Yoram wouldn't speak about Prime Minister Sharon's Disengagement Plan, and he had taken to going out on very long walks with Beauty in the sand dunes. Once Efrat had accompanied him, and Yoram had not said a word the entire time; just watched Beauty running happily over the dunes and stared sadly out at the blue-gray sea. Yair was very involved with the Anti Disengagement Committee. He had been the only one in the Yefet family to wear an orange Star of David, joined Miri one evening a week on her "door to door" and refused to even consider losing the-struggle-to-stay-in-Gush Katif.

"Of course we'll win, Effie," he had said last night, his hands unconsciously clenched into fists. "We'll win because we have to win; we know the danger that awaits the country if we don't."

"But," she had protested. "The government is against us, the media is against us and the courts are against us! How can we win against such powers?"

Yair had been silent for a bit and then he had said quietly: "We have the people on our side. The Jewish nation is with us! We're planning huge demonstrations, marches, a human chain – which will reach until Jerusalem! And some of us are even willing to block streets. Why, if Prime Minister Sharon doesn't change his mind, come summer we'll flood the Gush with tens of thousands of Jews from all over; throwing 8,000 Jews from their homes is one thing. Throwing 80,000 Jews is another thing." Yair's face had glowed as he anticipated the struggle to come and its happy conclusion.

"Then why is *Aba* so sad and quiet lately?"

Yair shrugged, "*Aba* doesn't figure we'll manage to get 80,000 people here. And he thinks that even if we do, Disengagement will still go through – it'll take the soldiers longer, but it'll go through. But hush," Yair added quickly, "not a word of this to anyone! You know how people here will feel if they hear such talk!"

Efrat nodded. She remembered how angry Mrs. Eisley had been at Miri because Miri didn't support wearing an orange Star of David.

"I am willing to do anything to stop Disengagement!" Mrs. Eisley had yelled.

"Well I have my boundaries," Miri had said calmly.

"But they want to make Gush Katif *Judenrein*!" Mrs. Eisley had sobbed.

"But they aren't Nazis," Miri said imperturbably.

"I never said that they were." And Mrs. Eisley had left in a huff.

Efrat was glad that her mother and Mrs. Eisley were good friends again.

Tu B'Shvat passed. Yair returned to Katif Yeshiva. Efrat continued studying and reading as usual.

22 Shvat (February 1)

Dear Mem,

On Thursday I was sitting in the Ulpana library finishing my English assignment – an essay about Tu B'Shvat. Happily, the librarian showed up (she hasn't been there for several days) and I checked out the book: Four Steps to the Gallows. It is edited by Arie Eshel, an Irgun (NMO) member himself, and includes all the letters written in jail by Irgun member Avshalom Haviv to his family and to his girlfriend Gila. I'd started reading it in the library and was very pleased to finally be able to check it out. Of course I spent all Shabbat reading it – and finished it. It really left an impression on me. In fact, I felt like I was invisible in the Acre prison, seeing but unseen. Hearing, but unheard. And watching those three brave Jews Avshalom Haviv, Ya'acov Weis and Meir Nakar living in the shadow of the gallows, and yet they were cheerful and strong; writing letters to family and friends, talking to each other and singing and even joking. And they spent months like that – knowing constantly that in as little as five minutes they could be hanged by the British.

Towards the end of the book, I started reading out loud and crying – I was moved so deeply. The description of their last few hours before the British hanged them; their calling out to their comrades, "Be strong, we will not shame," and their being hanged in the midst of singing HaTikva (which is now our National Anthem) which their comrades joined and continued… it chokes the throat.

And I wonder, would I have been able, in prison, to be "Ready for the worst but hoping," to tease my friend about her spelling mistakes, advise her and send cheerful letters to her and to my family? How does one prepare himself for the gallows at the age of twenty one?! I guess one must believe very strongly in the cause one is fighting for.

Tomorrow Yair will be joining the march. They will walk until S'derot. I think I'll join the second day of the march – it's a four day march from Gush Katif until Jerusalem, with a demonstration opposite the Prime Minister's house when we reach Jerusalem.

I've got an English test tomorrow on the story The Enemy. It's an interesting story, and I hope the test goes well.

I also need to print out the biology report saved on disc. Merav and I need to hand the report in by Monday.

My history quiz on Thursday (on the 1929 Arab riots) went very well, I think. Our teacher didn't seem to expect us to write a lot, but…I wrote a page and a half!

'Night,
Effie.

23 Shvat (February 2)

Dear Mem,
What a day!
The weather was horrid; very cold, strong cold winds (my eyes teared from the wind on my way to the Ulpana) and rain off and on.

We didn't study at all today. The Anti Disengagement Committee asked our grade to please make the display of the Gush that the marchers will present for the people of S'derot – urgent! We only had until 4:00 in the afternoon to make it. So… we worked on it non-stop all day.

We weren't that many girls – not more than thirty both twelfth grade classes combined, since some were marching, some were sick and some checking out National Service positions for next year.

The Ulpana "closed an eye" to the fact that we all weren't in

118

class... We went to the computers in the biology lab and down-loaded dozens and dozens of pictures from Katif.net. We really did a lovely job covering Gush Katif from every possible aspect: ideology, agriculture, education, tourist sites. Excellent!

Yair went on the march with his yeshiva. We saw him on the news this evening! He was marching and holding one end of a big banner. Poor fellow – it was raining and hailing and strong gusts of wind, yet they held the banners and marched. I was so proud seeing that yet it gave me a sad feeling too.

The police will only allow fifty people to march at a time. Horrid!

The weather is supposed to be better tomorrow, and I and nearly the entire Ulpana plan to go. There will be buses to take us to the starting point. It should be fun!

Effie

~~~

An essay for English class

En route to Ashkelon
By Efrat Yefet
25 Shvat (February 4)

It was Monday morning, 7:35, and I was walking quickly through the paths of Neve Dekalim. I quickened my pace; the bus taking us to the day's starting point was supposed to leave at 7:45 and I wanted to make sure I'd be there on time. The day before, a group of Gush Katif residents had marched from Kissufim to S'derot. They had very difficult weather conditions: wind, rain and hail, but they believed in their purpose and marched on – drenched and cold.

To see them walking in the rain and hail with signs and banners really made me understand how serious the situation is. Prime Minister Sharon keeps talking about ridding Gaza of Jews and the media is absolutely delighted with Sharon's intention of carrying out Unilateral Concessions!

So, Gush Katif decided to organize a four day protest march. The first day: marching from Kissufim to S'derot. The second day: marching from S'derot to Ashkelon. The third day: marching from Ashkelon to Kiryat Malachi. The fourth day: marching from Kiryat Malachi to Jerusalem where a demonstration will take place in the evening. Today is the second day and I will be marching from S'derot to Ashkelon.

My brother Yair had gone on the march yesterday. He returned late at night, soaking wet, and told us how the first day of the march had been.

When we reached S'derot, we took the signs and banners out of the buses, put on orange hats and bought orange shirts that had written on them: Gush Katif is marching forward.

After pretending to listen to a short speech about how we were to listen to the policemen escorting us, we started marching: men first, ladies second; modesty! The signs and banners were held up high and the orange Gush Katif flags, and blue and white flags of Israel fluttered in the breeze. Many vehicles that passed us honked in support. We started singing and chanting slogans. After some time, when we'd run out of ideas for a new song to sing, we just sang along with the tapes being played: a disc of the Katif Yeshiva band and a disc of the Gush Katif band Ma'arava MiKan. Those songs were peaceful and pleasant to listen to but they were NOT marching songs.

We continued walking. The police were making sure we didn't cross the yellow line and the reporters were trying to get a good shot. Some reporters rode in the back of the leading vehicle, some walked among us, and some actually climbed on top of the bus stop and sat there filming us as we marched past. We rather ignored them. The police did the same.

The view was lovely; all green fields, orchards and flowers. We stopped for lunch at Yad Mordechai. The *Ulpana* provided lunch; buns and spreads. We all started cheering the *Ulpana* and then settled down and ate. We rested there for about an hour. The men and boys started dancing in circles…

Finally we continued marching and reached Ashkelon. We were joined there by many more families from the Gush, and by nearly the entire community of Nitzarim. The ADC gave us all

stickers and fliers and divided us into groups. I stayed with the largest group and we walked to the *Midrachov*. It was pretty funny every time we had to cross a street; the young leader of our group had to remind us that we were there to sanctify G-d's name, not desecrate it!

We chanted slogans as we walked. Many people just stared at us, but a few said "*Yashar Koach!*" When we reached the *Midrachov* some of us stood in one spot while holding the signs and banners, while the others walked around the *Midrachov* handing out the fliers and stickers.

One elderly woman thought at first that we were protesting in order to get more money. I must admit, we were a really odd sight there; religious ideological youth dressed in Gush Katif orange, chanting, handing out stickers and fliers in an open air market place, when nearly everyone else who is there is secular and engrossed in their everyday life with its own problems.

Finally we walked from there to the Ashkelon *Matnas*, guided by Ashkelon youth. Drivers honked at us in support as they sped by us, and we waved back.

At the *Matnas*, the mayor of Ashkelon, the mayor of Gush Katif and the *Rav* of Nitzarim gave speeches. Then we saw a short film that the mass-media teacher had made about the Gush. The film was really good. It started off by showing the beauty of Gush Katif; the sea, the hot houses, the flourishing communities… then it showed the Navy radar at the beach spinning around and around, and the music turned threatening. Images flashed showing mortars exploding, ambulances rushing with sirens squealing and the doctor with an intense look of anger and pain on his keen face as he looks up from the killed Jew on the stretcher. Then the film interviewed several Gush Katif residents who were injured yet chose to keep on living in Gush Katif. The film ended showing a group of men dancing in the town center on Israel's Independence Day, with one man in the center of the rings waving a blue and white flag of Israel. Fireworks exploded in the dark night sky, and the flag was still seen waving in the background.

Afterwards the youth separated; some spending the night in Ashkelon (in the Ashkelon Yeshiva and *Ulpana* dorms), and some returned to the buses to return to the Gush.

We were a quiet group in the bus on the way home – each of us silently reliving the events of the eventful day.

Chapter 22

And so the month of Shvat (February) sped by. Efrat started worrying about where to do National Service next year. In fact, she didn't know what she wanted to work in during National Service.

"You should work in a library," Yair told her, chuckling.

"But I won't get to read the books," she objected. "I'll have to check them out for other people."

"You are so good in your studies, you should work in a school," Miri advised her.

But Efrat just shrugged and walked up the hill thinking. As she picked a long and slender dark-green leaf from an acacia tree growing next to the red and gray brick sidewalk, it came to her with a flash; she wanted to remain in the Gush next year! Efrat gazed at the golden sand dunes, at the red roofed houses, at the blue sea and at the palm fronds waving in the distance by the sea. She heard a spur winged plover call out sharply. Then she turned to the east and looked at the massive gray sprawl of naked cement buildings that was K'han Yunis. She shuddered and stiffened, her short slender form erect and straight like a sword's blade. She stood there, a proud, pretty figure alone on a hilltop staring at the ugly Arab city from which deadly mortars and kassam rockets were fired at her and at her community; in which the streets were filled with masked and unmasked Arabs shouting slogans, shooting rifles in the air; their dark glittering eyes and bold faces telling – as much as the burning epithets of the State of Israel and the pile of ashes that was once a bonny blue and white flag of the Jewish state – their desires and ambition of turning the Mediterranean Sea red with Jewish blood and erecting a "Palestine" on the ruins of Israel.

"I'm staying in Gush Katif," Efrat said out loud to the gray sprawl on the eastern horizon. And the words hung in the air like a threat and a promise.

"Yes," she said again, quietly but determined. "I'm staying here." She sank down onto the cool golden sand as if suddenly drained of all her energy. A fresh breeze from the sea blew her soft wavy brown hair back from her pretty face. A troubled look stole into her almond shaped brown eyes and she picked up a small twig and started breaking it into small pieces.

"Now," she said to herself, "I've decided where I'm doing National Service. All that is left is to decide what I'll be doing, and to get accepted."

She sat there, lost in thought. As the evening grew cooler, she rose to her feet, brushed the sand from her denim skirt and headed home.

"*Ima*," she called as she entered the house, "*Ima*, I've decided to stay in the Gush next year…"

Sunday, 18 Adar Aleph, 5765 (February 27, 2005)

Dear Mem,

I really like Celtic songs. I've been listening to a lot of them lately and they are lovely! The music and melodies are so hauntingly sad and sweet that it stirs your soul.

Mem, I've changed. Nowadays, when I get home from the Ulpana, I have very little patience to study; all I want to do is to indulge in my hobbies: read, walk in the sand dunes, listen to music… And yet I know that I can't afford to do so – I have tests coming up!

I spoke of it to Ima, explaining to her that lately I am able to concentrate on my books for hours, but I'm not able to concentrate on my homework. Ima said that I'm probably suffering from 'escapism'. I think she's right.

Today I went to the health clinic again – about National Service there next year. Oh, if only I'll be accepted! I'd like to work there next year – the people are nice and it would be interesting.

I have a lot to do tomorrow: water my neighbor's garden, study for a test I have on Tuesday, exercise… and my allergies are terrible! But, Mem, the acacias are blooming! And so are the

flowers! The rotems are lovely and the scent is so sweet!
Efrat.

(From Efrat's diary entry, we learn that she was trying to get accepted for National Service at the health clinic, and that she was suffering from "escapism.")

Yes, indeed. Efrat was, for the first time in her twelve years of school, having a difficult time concentrating on her schoolwork, and instead, she was sinking during her spare time into a pleasant world of books, sand dunes, and music.

Why was she behaving so? Well, when a person feels a need to escape, it is because that person is being chased. And Efrat was being chased. Relentlessly. She was being chased...by Disengagement.

Yes, around every corner; on the 6:00 evening news, during walks and talks with her brother Yair, while helping her mother with the household chores, on strolls in the sand dunes with her father and, hardest of all, during classes, the horrid topic of Disengagement always came up.

And since Efrat heard so much talk about Disengagement at her home, she extremely disliked hearing so much talk of it at school too. But it was inevitable; practically every class sooner or later into the lesson turned into yet another discussion of Disengagement.

For instance, several days ago, the first class had been Bible. The twelfth grade was learning the book of Eyov (Job). Enters the small elderly teacher, clicking sharply with her high heels. The girls dutifully open their notebooks, and Efrat opened her notebook too and held a pen poised in her right hand. The teacher took out her notes and her book from her brown leather satchel, put on her reading glasses and started the lesson.

"Right, girls. Good morning! Let's see... I'll review shortly. Last time we read about *Hashem* trying Eyov by bringing upon him one misfortune after another – starting with his animals and ending with his children. And he doesn't even have time to recuperate between the tragedies; while the first messenger is still telling him the bad things that have happened the second messenger already appears! And while the second messenger is still talking the third messenger comes!" The teacher paused and glanced sharply at the girls over her spectacles.

"Yeah," Ilanit says. "Rather like us; we are still trying to get used to mortars falling and shooting attacks on the road, when we suddenly learn from the media that Prime Minister Sharon has come up with an expulsion plan!"

Efrat groaned quietly, and closed her notebook and put the cap on her pen.

"And we're still trying to get used to this expulsion plan," Ilanit continued, "when we're told that the Minister of Education won't make stuff any easier for us on our end-of-year-exams!"

"What?!" Roni asked. "How do you know that?"

Ilanit grinned. "Why, yesterday Shosh and I had a meeting with the Minister. We were at the Knesset – that's why we weren't at school yesterday."

"And what did you say to her?" Rivka asked, as curious as all the other girls in the class.

Ilanit ran a hand through her smooth long brown hair. "We tried to explain to her the difficulties we are going through: mortars, Arab attacks, Disengagement… and," she continued angrily, "she didn't even care!"

"That's right," Shosh chimed in. "When the mortars first started falling, girls got ten extra points on their end-of-year-exams. Well the mortars haven't stopped, and things have gotten much worse, but no chance of us getting ten extra points…"

"How come? Why won't they give us some extra points? It's the only fair and decent thing to do," Rotem said.

"It's very simple," the *Tanach* teacher said. "The government wants all the Gush Katif youth to be busy inside their homes studying for exams, instead of being out and about fighting Disengagement. And they'll do all they can to achieve that – fair and decent or not."

"They won't succeed," Ilanit scoffed. "Who cares about exams? Saving our homes is much more important!"

There was a loud murmur of assent in the twelfth grade classroom.

The Tanach teacher shook her head. "No, my dear, that is the wrong attitude. When this year is over, whether Disengagement happens or not (please G-d, may it not happen) you all will need to have passed your exams. Otherwise you won't be accepted to any university! You think the Minister cares about your futures? You think Ariel Sharon is worried about your finding a job? Each and every one of you girls needs to worry about yourselves as well as worry about the Land. I'm not saying that you should only study and forget about our struggle to keep Gush Katif. No indeed! I am saying that you need to act wisely, maturely. So maybe your grades won't be as high as they could have been. Maybe you'll do four points English instead of five points, but pass your exams! Don't let Prime Minister Sharon and his government ruin your futures!" The Tanach teacher spoke earnestly.

Ilanit nodded. "I understand what you're saying. For me, my home comes first and my exams come second. My exams are important to me – otherwise I wouldn't bother coming to classes…"

"Me too," Rachel agreed smiling. "Anti Disengagement Committee comes first, exams second. At least once a week I go 'door to door'. And the Anti Disengagement Committee keeps asking me to go speak in this kibbutz, that high school –"

"This Knesset meeting…" Ilanit chimed in.

"What Knesset meeting?" Rivka asked curiously. "You didn't tell us!"

"Oh, didn't I?" Ilanit asked innocently, her eyes twinkling.

"What's this?" The Tanach teacher asked with interest. "You spoke in the Knesset?"

"Yes, some Knesset committee. You see," Ilanit launched into an explanation, "I got this phone call:

- *Hello, this is Reuvan Tal. Am I speaking with Ilanit?*

- *Yes, this is Ilanit. And stop kidding! You think I don't know your voice, David?*

- *Hello Ilanit. I would like you to please represent Gush Katif in our Knesset committee that is meeting this week. I think it important that my colleagues hear what you have to say; as a resident of Gush Katif.*

- *Oh, come on! Stop teasing me David. So, David, why did you call?*

127

- *Ilanit, I assure you, this is Reuvan Tal speaking.*
- *Really???*
- *Yes.*
- *Oh my goodness. Oops!!*
- *So will you attend the meeting?*
- *Um, yeah. Sure. What time do I need to be there?*

So, on Monday when I got to the Knesset (that's why I got to the *Ulpana* only in the late afternoon that day) the guards didn't want to let me in at first – because I couldn't find my identity card! And I started to really worry, because the meeting was about to begin!"

"Oh, my!" the class gasped.

"So what happened?" the Tanach teacher asked sharply.

Ilanit laughed. "Reuvan Tal had to send his personal secretary to sign that I was who I claimed to be, and that Reuvan Tal would be responsible for me. Then I was allowed in, and I had to keep walking really fast and keep asking people for directions. It was a real miracle that I got there about five minutes before I was supposed to start speaking."

"And what did you say?" Rivka asked.

The whole class was silent, waiting for Ilanit's answer.

"What did I say?" Ilanit sighed. "I spoke about my love for my community; the wonderful people, the hothouses, the Jews that were killed as the price for settling the land. I spoke of my parents – they were among the founders of our community. My father has grown vegetables for years. My father hires Arabs, he speaks their language. We aren't fanatics or extremists. And now, I see my father crying in the kitchen. He keeps asking my mother what we will do if there is Disengagement. What will happen to our hothouses? He's fifty three years old – he can't start anew.

"Ilanit, you really saw your father crying?" Rivka asked gently, surprised.

"My father was crying the other day too," Hadar admitted reluctantly.

"Really, what will our parents do if Disengagement happens – no hot houses, they can't just find a new job..." Tamar said earnestly.

"Quiet!" Roni suddenly demanded. "Stop talking like this! Disengagement won't happen," she said seriously in her sweet voice.

Several girls laughed.

"I hope it won't – I really, really, really, hope it won't. And I'm doing all I can so that it won't," Ilanit said. "But what if it does?" she asked.

Just then the bell rang and her question went unanswered. Yet even if everyone had heard her question, who could have answered it? Even Prime Minister Ariel Sharon couldn't have answered it.

The Tanach teacher picked up her leather satchel. "Ilanit, do you have your speech written down? I'd like to read it."

"Sure. I'll give you a copy of the protocol of the meeting."

What Ilanit had to say was interesting, Efrat thought to herself. But I am sick of Disengagement. Sick of it! Can't we even learn one lesson without being sidetracked and distracted? And Efrat's thoughts are somewhat excusable since that had been the seventh lesson that week and the umpteenth lesson that month in which the class's studies had been disrupted. And we have end-of-year-exams this year too! she thought furiously.

Chapter 23

Champagne Returns

By Boaz Ha'atzani, Adar 5765 (March 2005)
[Translated from the Hebrew by Shifra Shomron.
BeSheva Newspaper, with permission.]

"To chop settlers' hands." (Ehud Olmert)

"To break their hands and legs," "Don't be too nice." (Prime Minister Ariel Sharon)

"The inner enemy is more dangerous than Arafat or Assad... to press the trigger slowly, responsibly, coldly and smartly." (MK Avshalom Vilin)

"Even if it means bloodshed." (Yoel Marcus).

"Civil war doesn't frighten me." (Moshe Negby).

[And the author of this article brings many more similar quotes which I'll spare my readers – S. Shomron]

Incitement is being spouted and it is encouraging illegitimate deeds. [...] While in the right wing camp there isn't a *Rav* or a leader calling for violence, the incitement, the hate and the cruel style in the left wing comes from the leaders and the elite. One can also see the rivers of hate every day in the left wing responses on the internet. [...]

What is the purpose of the current wave of incitement?

Sharon and his comrades and the media which is at their disposal are achieving several purposes. The immediate one is showing his opposers as criminals, defaming and scaring them, in order to banish the legitimacy of demanding a referendum from beneath their feet. Another purpose of the offensive campaign is creating a smoke screen around the easy release of hundreds of murderous Arabs back to the streets: thus the future victims are busy defending their good name, and haven't the ability to criticize the resurrection of the terror backbone. At the same opportunity the *Shabak* is also silenced from crying out against the release, and instead is incited to a different purpose: the "extreme right." [...]

Their main purpose is to frighten and deter us from struggling for our homes. From our perspective, we need to fulfill their greatest nightmare – not fear at all.

~~~

Efrat finished reading the article and closed the newspaper. She pressed her small slender fingers against her temples which were throbbing painfully from the article she'd just read.

How can they hate us so? She wondered. Don't they realize that it is all of us, the Jewish Nation, against the Arab enemy?! But no, instead they release murderers and send their poisonous barbs at us! She was disgusted. What a stupid people, and yet they are dangerous too. She shuddered slightly.

Tiredly she rose and started making herself a cup of hot chocolate, her favorite beverage when she had a headache.

Just then Yair entered the kitchen. Many different emotions were swiftly dashing across his handsome face: incredibility, anger, amusement…

"Effie," he cried out loudly. "You'll never believe what some friends from *Yeshiva* just told me!"

Efrat groaned, "Yair, quiet please. I have a terrible headache. Just read something really rotten –"

"Oops, sorry," Yair said more softly, his eyes dancing excitedly and he hastily drew up a chair. "It's like this: the *Shabak* is trying to recruit us!" And he sat back to enjoy the shocked look on Efrat's face. "A classmate of mine accepted a ride to *Yeshiva* in a white civilian car that had stopped by him. Inside were several men – all of them wearing dark sunglasses. Anyhow, the men admitted to being *Shabak* agents and tried to convince my friend to help them. At first they tried to persuade him by saying that they were both on the same side – both trying to prevent a civil war. Well, my friend quickly retorted: 'Who said I want to prevent a civil war?!' So then they tried to bribe him; offered him a salary, a cell phone, to pay his fuel costs…"

"But this is crazy!" Efrat interrupted. "What do we even have knowledge of that the *Shabak* are so eager to learn from us? As if a teenager here knows any deep dark secrets?!"

"Don't you understand?" Yair asked excitedly. "It isn't what we know, it's what they think we know. For months now the *Shabak* has been inciting against us and warning the public to fear us. They are trying to make us all look like extremists. They're convinced that we have plans to blow up the mosque on the Temple Mount, or massacre Arabs, or assassinate Sharon... and they figure that it'll be carried out by hot headed youth. Well, on their own the *Shabak* has tried to get wind of these plans that they are convinced exist. And they have failed to get wind of any such plans," Yair grinned. "'Cause these plans don't exist. But they don't realize that, or they just refuse to admit that. They figure that we're keeping our cards super close to our chest. So now they're willing to try bribery in order to get some youth in Gush Katif to be spies for them."

"Goodness, how scary! I hope they don't approach me!" Efrat exclaimed.

Yair nodded. "Don't accept a ride from anyone you don't know and if some strange men bother you on the street – just ignore them or threaten to call the police. That's what the *Rav* at our *Yeshiva* told us to do."

"Has only one student at your *Yeshiva* been confronted by the *Shabak?*"

"No, several have. I think five, no six."

~~~

Revealing: The Shabak is Trying to Recruit Gush Katif Youth

BeSheva Newspaper, 27 Adar Bet 5765 (April 7th 2005)
[Translated from the Hebrew by Shifra Shomron, with permission.]

The Gush Katif youth have lately become preferred recruits by *Shabak* agents. The organization's choice way of action is to offer the youth a ride and during the ride to try and convince them to become *Shabak* agents.

One of the girls, who received such an offer tells: "A civilian vehicle offered me a ride in the direction of Neve Dekalim and, during the ride, offered me to aid the *Shabak* in order to 'prevent a civil war and bloodshed.'"

Another youth was asked to report on demonstrations and

"events of youth from the Gush that are not within the law."

After the youth refused the offers, the *Shabak* people tried to seduce them through promises. Among other things they offered the youth a salary, a cell phone and even a car.

~~~

Yair was quiet and Efrat finished drinking her hot chocolate. Yoram walked into the kitchen.

"Hello. Bad day today. We weren't allowed into the B'dolach hothouses until midday because there were warnings of Arab infiltrations to that area." Yoram sighed. "Well, what's up? Anything new at *Yeshiva*, Yair?"

Efrat glanced at her father's weary face. He looked tired, drained. His very shoulders sagged. She shot Yair a quick warning look.

"No, nothing special," Yair answered. "Just what's expected."

Yoram nodded absently, and sank into a comfortable reclining chair. Just then the front door burst open and Miri strode furiously into the house.

"My goodness, have you heard?!" She demanded angrily, her every word shooting out like a bullet.

"Uh oh," Efrat thought. "She's heard about the *Shabak* agents, and now Yair and I will have to listen to an hours worth of warnings."

"The cemetery!"

"Huh?" Efrat wondered out loud.

"Our filthy, our rotten, our, our," Miri stuttered, trying to find words to express her disgust and strong anger. "Our wretched government is already planning to dig up the bodies in the cemetery!"

The room was silent following this horrific statement.

"I don't understand," Yoram said, his forehead furrowed.

Miri tried to explain: "I was just at the Eisleys and apparently the army asked the Moatza (regional council) for the keys to the cemetery. The army wanted to count how many graves there are to take out." Miri paused for a second, and her generally merry brown eyes now flashed angrily. A shudder ran up Efrat's spine as she heard the word "graves."

Miri continued, "The army has started its preparations for Disengagement. Not only will they have to banish the 8,000 Jews living in Gush Katif, they'll also have to dig up our loved ones." Miri started sobbing and Efrat was shocked to see her mother's face covered in tears. Yoram put a comforting arm around his wife. Yair stared down at the floor, his hands clenched in fists.

"And the, the bereaved families," Miri continued her voice muffled against Yoram's shoulder, "they are so shocked and so angry! And they're trying to get the High Court to rule that the army won't be allowed to remove the bodies before the families are removed."

"You know," Yair said quietly to Efrat. "If the bodies are dug up, all the families will have to sit in mourning again."

Efrat looked at her sobbing mother. She'd never seen her mother cry before; Miri was always so light hearted and merry. Yoram was still hugging his wife. His face looked stern and sad. Efrat noticed some more gray hair in his beard.

Everything seemed so crazy; *Shabak* agents trying to recruit Gush Katif youth, the army planning to dig up the Gush Katif cemetery, her mother sobbing…

Efrat couldn't take it any longer. She stood up abruptly and left the house. Aimlessly she wandered through the garden; walking silently on the green grass, around the sturdy shade trees and next to the thick hedge. Finally she stood still, leaned against the brown trunk of a shade tree and watched the beautiful sunset. Yair came out and joined her as the burning orb sank into the blue sea.

"The struggle has only begun, Effie. Don't worry; the High Court will delay the order regarding digging up the graves, and we haven't played all our cards yet either."

Efrat sighed. "I know you mean to comfort me, Yair, but you don't. I just wish it was all over – for good or for bad, but at least done with!"

Yair opened his mouth to retort, but closed it again when he saw how troubled his sister's face was. He thought of his mother crying in the living room, and of the families anxiously waiting for the High Court's decision, and he wondered if he didn't perhaps agree with his sister.

The last sun's rays disappeared and darkness descended. Efrat and Yair sat quietly and watched.

~~~

Several days later a large prayer vigil was held near the main street and the wide lawn of the two large Neve Dekalim synagogues.

Efrat and Yair walked up the hill in order to look down on the gathering.

"Wow, look at all the people that came – the street is really full!" Efrat enthusiastically exclaimed.

"Quiet," Yair admonished her. "I want to hear them blow the silver trumpets that they brought specially from *Machon HaMikdash*."

"But you know Yair, this all seems rather pathetic. Prime Minister Ariel Sharon is busy training the army to drag us from our homes, and all we do is gather to say psalms and blow silver trumpets!"

"Effie," Yair said sternly, "we don't know what will induce *Hashem* to help us in our struggle to keep the land He gave us. We do know though, that *Hashem* commanded us to blow the silver trumpets in times of danger and of war."

Efrat felt ashamed at her cynical outburst. She knew that her brother was right.

Just then the clear music of the trumpets rang out. Again and again. Loud and long and clear. Efrat felt something stir in her and stood still and proud; only her heart whispered to *Hashem*: "*Hashem* please, you chose us as your nation, redeemed us from the Egyptian bondage and gave us the Holy Land of Israel. Please, *Hashem*, help us keep this land! Help us defeat our enemies, obey your commandments and keep our land!" A tear barely seen trickled down her soft cheek. A plover called out sharply in the rose colored evening sky overhead.

"*To the Chief Musician, A Psalm of David. How long wilt thou forget me O Lord? Forever? How long wilt thou hide thy face from me? How long shall take counsel in my soul, having sorrow in my heart daily? How long shall my enemy be exalted over me? Look, and hear me, O Lord my G-d: lighten my eyes, lest I sleep the sleep of death; lest my enemy say, I have prevailed against him; and those who trouble me rejoice when I am moved.*

But I have trusted in thy mercy; my heart shall rejoice in thy salvation. I will sing to the Lord, because he has dealt bountifully with me." *[Psalms 13]*

Chapter 24

Dear Mem,

Merav didn't get accepted to National Service in Be'er Sheva. I feel sorry for her. Thank goodness I got accepted for National Service in the health clinic here in Neve Dekalim!

Some fifty (!) mortars fell during Shabbat. A horse belonging to a family that lives in the villa neighborhood by the Ulpana was killed. Sad. Thank goodness no Jew was hurt! It's been some time since we had mortars.

A Knesset Member bought a house in one of the four settlements in the Northern Shomron that the government also intends to destroy during Disengagement. Well, if Gush Katif falls, than those four Northern Shomron settlements don't have a chance.

Yair finished composing his first melody. It is really lovely; solemn, sweet and sad. And we found words for it too – a verse from psalms. Absolutely perfect!

The weather today was hot and dry – real hamsin weather. Horrid! Out in the sand dunes Aba, Beauty, Rufus, and I walked to "the meadow." Of course it is all brown there now. Beauty saw a hole and after sticking her nose in it, started digging furiously. After a bit, Aba helped her and a few minutes later called me to see…the head of a monitor lizard peeking out at us! The monitor lizard was scared and hissing loudly. Aba managed to get it out – all seventy centimeters of it. Huge! And a bit scary for me. We had to chain the dogs to a nearby acacia tree, because they were very excited over the monitor lizard and kept getting too near for safety. The monitor lizard's claws are very long and sharp, and it could have easily hurt the dogs.

After examining it closely, we let it scramble away over the fallen brown leaves and over the sand. We figure that it'll dig itself a new den since we discovered its old den. Amazing animal; it really looked very dinosaur like.

Efrat.

Monday, the week of Passover

Dear Mem,
I am soooo busy – so much studying to do! I have a matconit (a test given by the teacher before the end-of-year-exams given by the Board of Education) in Oral law the week I return to school. And I wasn't feeling so well today. Tough!

On the night of the Passover Seder, we all dressed up as ancient Hebrews. It was a lot of fun! I wore a scarf and held a staff. Of course we all wore sandals. Aba and Yair wrapped shirts around their heads and tied the sleeves in back. Ima wore a long gown with a sash tied in the middle. Our dress-up really created the right atmosphere for the reading of the Hagada.

Wednesday, the week of Passover

Dear Mem,
So, I have finished studying the last two chapters of Oral Law. Finally!

Last night we lost electricity. It was a real bother. We all went to bed early.

When I was eating lunch today outside on the dead grass (yes, you read correctly – dead grass! Aba is so convinced Disengagement will happen that he has nearly stopped watering the lawn. It is terribly depressing. Ima has insisted that he still water the trees and hedges; we can always replant the grass, but trees and hedges take years...), Yair and I found out that a kassam rocket had fallen at a neighbor's house, and hadn't exploded. Well, about seven types of security cars roared up, and smug officers and soldiers were standing stupidly around the unexploded rocket. Yair and I ignored them and kept on eating lunch, but a large soldier peered over our hedge and asked us 'kids' to 'please go inside'. How is that for house arrest? After some fifteen minutes, Yair and

The kassam

I got bored and we decided to join the Neve Dekalim Chol HaMoed activity; and walk down to the lake.

The way there was very crowded. And all types of people too: old, young, religious, secular... I suspect that many of them came just in order to see Gush Katif before, G-d forbid, Sharon gives it away.

Well, we joined the crowd and were about half way to the lake – we had reached the part where you have to pass between Arab houses, when two mortars fell fifteen meters away from Yair and from me. I froze. I just stood still and stared as the mortars exploded and sand and dust flew upwards. I was very scared. I really expected more mortars to fall – after all, a large Jewish crowd makes an excellent target.

I was very annoyed that no one in the crowd realized that mortars had just exploded by us. A few people halted and looked around, but continued without noticing anything.

Well, I was scared and annoyed. Yair was amused. "Watch, Effie, look at the soldiers. This should be interesting..."

I watched the four soldiers carefully step from their jeep, glance nervously at the crowd, and then – holding their guns shoulder height – walk into the brush. So stupid! What did they expect to do? The Arabs had fired the missiles and returned to the Arab village. Mission accomplished…

Yair and I continued walking. Now we had to pass by Arabs sitting in front of their houses. I was furious! My hands were clenched in fists… I was determined not to show what a scare I'd had.

On the way back home, Yair and I saw patrols of 3 to 4 soldiers. They were laughing, slouching; no heightened alertness about them.

When we told Aba the story he wasn't surprised; he's expected an attack on that road for years.

Effie.

24 Nissan, 5765 (May 3, 2005)

Dear Mem,
*Well, we're back at school – have been since yesterday. It seems as though we'll be kicked out from the Gush; American President George Bush supports it and Prime Minister Sharon is pushing it forwards full steam. And WHAT can we really do to stop it? I'm furious of course, and the worst thing is the sickening feeling of helplessness and apathy that's taken over. True, we haven't been idle: we've had demonstrations, signs at intersections, fliers, interviews, prayer vigils, 'face to face'. *sigh* Mem, just between you and me, the only way to stop Disengagement is a full scale rebellion.*

The Eisleys are constantly being interviewed, and they are really really good at it. We got so excited when we saw them on the news last night.

26 Nissan, 5765 (May 5, 2005)

Dear Mem,
Today is Holocaust Memorial Day. At the Ulpana we were shown a shocking film about second and third generation descendants of Holocaust survivors. These descendents are busy trying to prove that their parents / grandparents were born in Germany in order to receive a German passport, which they'll switch to a

European passport. And we are talking about thousands of Jews! Several parents/ grandparents were interviewed and they were shocked and very hurt that their grandchildren want to return to Germany/ Europe after all the atrocities done to them there. It is very sad.

We all stood for the siren at 10:00. I like the thought that all of Israel comes to a halt for one moment and stands in remembrance. And the memory should obligate us in the future!

What still shocks me the most is reading about the apathy of fellow Jews towards their brothers during the Holocaust. For example, I recently read an article in the BeSheva newspaper which talked about a Swedish Jewish woman who helped save Jews who fled from Germany during the Holocaust. And she stated during the interview that her major adversary was the leader of the Joint!

You know, Mem, I HATE the sense of, well, the shadow of gloom, the cloud of dread that is hanging over the Gush. People are active and positive, but it is there, it exists and it is felt.

I need to go water at my neighbor's.

Efrat.

Chapter 25

And so the month of Nissan passed by and the month of Iyar (May) dawned upon the world. Yoram started reading on the internet what SELA, the government organization appointed to aid future Gaza and Northern Shomron evacuees, had to say. He started figuring out how much compensation they would get for their 180 square meter house and half dunam garden. And then there were all the documents he needed – you had to prove to SELA that the center of your life really was in Gush Katif. Yoram started compiling a file; filling it with old electric bills, old water bills, hospital birth certificates, his kids' report cards showing they learned in Gush Katif schools, etc. Yoram didn't confide what he was doing to anyone; time enough for that later.

Meanwhile, Miri still did "face-to-face" at least three times a week. Like most of the Gush Katifnics, she was convinced that SELA was evil and refused to have anything to do with them. Soldiers had now been prohibited from eating at families in the Gush, but Miri and Mrs. Eisley baked cakes every Thursday and took them to the soldiers at the Kissufim junction. While there, they would also try and convince soldiers to disobey Disengagement orders. Now, this was a complete change in the settlers' attitude towards the army. For years, the settlers had viewed the Israel Defense Forces as something holy, and had worshipped it like the golden calf. For years they had worked hard to enter the elite combat units. For years the women had made hot soups for the soldiers on cold nights, and brought fruit and cakes on spring days. But now the settlers realized that the army was to be the tool used for their destruction, and the call to refuse orders became more and more accepted in the Religious Zionist camp. Fliers were distributed showing that well-known and greatly admired settler Rabbis all agreed that when it comes to destroying Jewish settlements soldiers must refuse orders. And only one well-known Rabbi publicly said to obey orders. Religious soldiers were confused. Most Rabbis refused to say clearly whether one is permitted or not permitted to obey orders. And therefore, *Rav* Shapira's greatness became even greater since this righteous elderly *Rav* was the only *Rav* who stressed in every single demonstration that the Jewish law forbids obeying orders in such a situation.

Every week the BeSheva newspaper published the names and numbers of active soldiers and reserve soldiers who had made it clear to their commanders that they would have nothing to do with executing Disengagement. But the numbers were small; three or four every week, and most of them reserve soldiers.

As for Efrat, well, it's a bit harder to say what she thought. After the first time, she neither joined her mother going "face-to-face" nor attended every single demonstration and prayer vigil. To tell the truth, Efrat was rather inclined to agree with her father that it was a lost cause. Efrat knew that demonstrations, prayer vigils, "face-to-face," and a couple dozen guys refusing orders wouldn't stop the Prime Minister obsessed with his dark and deadly Disengagement plan. As such views were not popular in the Gush, Efrat kept them to herself. Is it possible that the Gush will fall without a real struggle? She wondered. Gush Katifnics are calm people with great respect for the law. It is difficult to rouse them even when their houses and land are at stake. The Gush people attended demonstrations, hosted several prayer vigils, went "door-to-door," and recited Psalms with their young children every afternoon at four o'clock. No, Efrat came to a decision. If Gush Katif is to be saved, it'll be by our brothers living on the strong stony hills of Judea and Shomron. Their youth are used to struggling against army and police, and they are strong like the land they live on. We resemble our land too; sand, that molds itself to fit whoever steps on it! Efrat filled her days with her schoolwork, walks in the sand dunes and books. She disliked talking or listening to anything connected to Disengagement.

And now we have reached the last member of the Yefet family: Yair. Yair, like some other Gush Katif youths, was sick of the Anti Disengagement Committee and had left them. "They are too moderate," he'd complained to Efrat. "Their slogan is: With Love

We Will Win, and all they want us to do is 'face-to-face' and distribute products from Gush Katif. Well, I prefer spending my evenings talking to soldiers and trying to convince them to refuse orders. I and several other guys go to Kissufim every night." Yair had chuckled. "I bet you that the ADC would have been furious at our talk of refusing orders if *Rav* Shapira hadn't come out so publicly and endorsed it. He's a great man, you know. The only leader we seem to have now and he is ninety something years old!"

Regarding his school work, Yair wasn't concerned. "Oh, heck. It's a crazy year and we aren't learning much at *Yeshiva*. I'll just have to fix my end-of-the-year exams next year."

"Yair," Efrat questioned him one clear Iyar night. "Why aren't there more soldiers refusing orders? At least, all the religious soldiers ought to refuse orders!"

Yair thought a moment before replying. "Well, Effie, they don't see it as simply as we do. First of all, they are being brainwashed in the army, and it's getting more intense the closer we get to the date set for Disengagement. Also, if they refuse orders they'll be put on trial, sentenced to 28 days in jail, lose their army rank and they might even be thrown out from the army. And then there are all the guys that have made the army their career – they've signed contracts. They can't afford to refuse orders – they'll lose their jobs and won't be able to support their families. I can almost find it in me to pity them."

"Pity them?!" Efrat echoed, shocked. "I have no pity for a Jew who would rather throw Jews from their homes than lose his job!"

Yair nodded. "That's how we try to put it to the soldiers we talk to at Kissufim."

"Show me what you do," Efrat asked her brother curiously.

"Fine. Let's pretend you are the soldier."

Efrat nodded in agreement and her eyes twinkled.

"Hello, brother!" Yair shook her hand. "So where are you from?"

"I'm from Jerusalem."

"I've got a lot of friends from there. So how much longer do you have to serve?"

Efrat sighed. "Another year."

"Another year, well, you'd be surprised how quickly a year can pass. So, brother, what do you plan to do about Disengagement?"

"It's a terrible thing. How Sharon came up with this plan is beyond me…"

"Are you going to drag me from my house? Are you going to destroy my father's livelihood? Are you going to make my mother cry?"

The words were full of pain and came like bullets.

"Well, um, I," Efrat stammered, "look, I'm just a regular soldier. I have to do what I'm told to do."

"So you don't have a brain? You can't think for yourself?"

"Hey, I'm just a soldier. If I don't do it, someone else will – it'll still happen. So why should I face jail and a big mess if it's going to happen anyways?"

"Why? Because you are a man, and you, only you, are responsible for what you do. You'll be the one with the nightmares of dragging a young mother and her children from their home. You'll be the one who caused great pain to the Holocaust survivors who have been dragged from their homes before – but never by Jews. You'll be the one –"

"Look, I get your point. I'll think it over, O.K."

"Think it over. I'll be back tomorrow night, brother." And Yair shook Efrat's hand again.

"So that's what you guys say. Well, I expect you do get them to think it over at least."

"That's all we can do," Yair answered. "If we see a religious soldier, we quote *Rav* Shapira and argue from a religious point of view. Very few soldiers, religious or secular, want to drag Jews from their homes. They feel that they don't have a choice though. And our job is to convince them that the choice is theirs, and the responsibility is theirs."

Efrat was silent.

Yair gazed at the sickle moon that had just emerged from behind a dark cloud. "You know, Effie, there are a lot of people that are just hoping for a miracle; hoping that at the last minute something will happen which will stop Disengagement."

"Yes," Efrat smiled mockingly. "I know: that Sharon will change his mind, or that there'll be a national referendum or that all the soldiers will refuse orders…"

Yair shook his head. "No, many of them haven't even thought what the miracle will be – they're just convinced that there will be one."

"Foolish people."

"Can't you understand them, Effie?"

Efrat rose from the white plastic chair she was sitting on and walked a few steps forward. She looked at the black paved roads, the wide brick sidewalks, the dunams and dunams of gray hothouses in the nearby *Moshav* of Gadid, and the sturdy comfortable houses of all their neighbors. Lastly, she looked at the tall shade trees in their garden, the thick hedges and the small fruit on the citrus trees. A spur winged plover gave three short trills. She smiled ruefully. "Yes, Yair. I understand them. I want a miracle so badly that I can almost convince myself that there will be one. If there isn't a miracle then all this which is precious and mine and steeped with memories will be destroyed. My G-d, how can it be destroyed?! It doesn't seem possible that all the synagogues, houses, gardens and Shuls and schools will be destroyed! That this lovely oasis will be reduced to dry grains of sand! So there'll have to be a miracle to save Gush Katif."

Yair nodded. "Yes, that's the mindset."

A tear rolled down Efrat's soft cheek. "Fools," she said again, sadly.

3 Iyar, 5765 (May 12, 2005)

Dear Mem,

Yesterday, Memorial Day for the fallen soldiers was hard. We all went to the Gush Katif cemetery. A lot of people were there, and soldiers were there too; some in olive green but also fifteen Navy officers in their handsome spotless white uniforms. We all stood when the siren went off (the soldiers all snapping to attention), and afterwards were several speeches. The most touching speech was the one given by a bereaved mother. You could have heard a pin drop when she cried out, my child! I will do everything I can so that you aren't dug up from your grave! You loved the sea…

I don't think there was a dry eye left by the time a bereaved father stepped forward to say Kaddish. His son, a young soldier, had been killed by the Arabs not that long ago while preventing an Arab infiltration into the community of Morag. His voice shook as he recited Kaddish, and I was afraid he wouldn't be able to finish it. The women around me were all weeping, and I was blinking hard so as not to cry also.

Well, the number of Jews killed in wars and other Arab attacks in Israel now stands at 21,954. And while the Rav is fond of saying that we must see it in its proper proportions; fifty-seven years of statehood in which the number of killed Jews equals one day at Auschwitz, I don't agree with his proportions. You see, Mem, when we have the means to defend ourselves, even one Jew being killed is inexcusable. And more than 1,000 Jews have been killed in the past five years, because, though the Arabs are at open war with us, all we do is bomb empty buildings and empty fields. It's as if we are aiding the Arabs in killing us!

Independence eve. Yair, Natanel, Rotem and I stayed together. The band playing in the town center wasn't very good (except for a short while when they played country music), so we kept walking around, staying near but not quite in the town center. On one of these rounds I saw the well-known fiery leader of a well-known right-wing organization walking just ahead of us along with her family. As we passed them I welcomed her to Gush Katif. Well, if she's moved to the Gush, I predict that Yair is going to be busy...

Yair and I returned home at about midnight, so as to see the fireworks from our house. They were absolutely gorgeous! But they sounded like mortars and I kept flinching every time one exploded.

Poor Beauty was terrified; she was sure that the loud BOOMS were mortars, and frantically tried to get out of her pen – clawing at the gate and howling. Aba let her out of the pen so she could be with us and feel safer but she dashed into the house at once... Well, Ima didn't allow her to be in the house, so Yair was trying to calm Beauty down outside the house when a big firework burst and Beauty leapt over the hedge and didn't stop running! So we scattered all over Neve Dekalim hunting for her. We even walked

*out into the sand dunes and called her name and offered treats, but
to no avail. Finally we gave up and returned home. The next
morning a neighbor of ours brought Beauty back to our house,
saying that Beauty had been hanging around her house looking
exhausted.*

*At noon Aba, Yair and I walked down to the lake. Ima was
visiting at the Eisleys and planned to meet us down there later.
There were many people, but not as many as we'd hoped for. Still,
it was a fun walk. Practically everyone was wearing orange, and
there were some people who had actually tied orange streamers on
their dogs! We were pleased to see some Hareidi men in their
traditional black hats and robes with some bright orange streamers
wrapped around their hat brims. Oh, Mem! If only we'd been
able to persuade the Hareidim to join us in our struggle to keep the
land of Israel, what a strong force we would be! The problem with
the Hareidim is that the majority of them are not nationalistic.
They ignore the mitzvah of settling the land of Israel and believe
that we shouldn't do a thing until the Redemption comes. It's a
shame.*

Efrat.

The seventh day of the month of Iyar (May 16) was a changing day in the lives of many in the State of Israel.

For the Yefet family it started out like any other day; Yoram
went to check some B'dolach hothouses, Miri went to the grocery
store to do some shopping, Efrat walked to the *Ulpana* and Yair was
at the Katif Yeshiva. The weather was lovely. The sky was clear
and the sea was blue.

Efrat came home that evening to find her parents watching
the television screen intently. Yoram was grinning widely and cheering: "Am Israel Chai, Am Israel Chai – yes! The people of Israel
are alive!"

"Effie, come see!" Miri called her over. "Three hundred and
fifty people have been arrested!"

"What? Why? Jews or Arabs?!" Efrat asked, bewildered.

"Jews!!! Mostly youth," Her father clarified. "They blocked
roads all over the country in order to protest against the Disengagement Plan, and show that if Gush Katif is shut down then the

whole country will be shut down!"

Tears filled Efrat's eyes. So people did care – cared enough to block roads and get arrested. If hundreds were arrested, that meant that thousands had showed up. And not for a peaceful demonstration; rather for a massive blocking of roads. "G-d bless them," she said earnestly.

Yoram was beaming. "They outsmarted the police and stopped the traffic for an hour in Jerusalem, Tel-Aviv, Be'er Sheva, Haifa and lots of other places. It's a huge success! And the Beit Leumi (National Home) organization has warned that this was only an experiment, and that when the real thing happens thousands will be arrested!"

Yoram got up.

"Where are you going?" Efrat asked.

"To water the lawn. I want to have a beautiful garden in time for the celebration feast we'll have when Disengagement fails!" And he went out whistling.

Miri and Efrat laughed and turned back to the television.

Later that night the phone rang. "Hello," Miri cheerfully answered. And then suddenly: "You what?!"

Efrat looked up in alarm.

"Well, where are you?! Call me again as soon as you can!" Miri hung up, and turned towards Efrat. "Efrat, your brother participated in blocking the road at the entrance to the capital. He's been arrested!"

"My goodness!" And the worried look upon Efrat's face mirrored the anxiety on Miri's face perfectly.

Miri slowly walked to the door. "I must tell Yoram," she said heavily.

Half an hour later, when Yoram and Miri reentered the house, Yoram was still angry. "I don't understand – we send the boy to *Yeshiva* and he goes to block roads without even calling to tell us first, without asking permission?! And how did the *Yeshiva* let them go without their parents' permission?!"

"*Aba*, please calm down. Yair certainly couldn't have foreseen that he would be arrested." Efrat grinned, "He didn't call to ask for permission probably because he knew you and *Ima* wouldn't allow him to go by himself. As for the *Yeshiva's* lack of supervision – well, that's ridiculous. I'm sure Yair's not the only one who snuck away from Katif Yeshiva to block roads. The *Yeshiva* probably told the boys not to go without permission and Yair went anyway..."

Yoram nodded. "Well, we should be proud of Yair. If only I wasn't so worried! I feel guilty for not having been there along with Yair; blocking roads isn't a kid's game."

And Miri and Efrat agreed.

Yair didn't call again that night, and the Yefet family anxiously awaited the eight o'clock morning news:

"Good morning and welcome to I.B.N. news broadcasting in Jerusalem. Last night over four hundred Israelis were arrested while committing acts of country wide civil disobedience, in which thirty major thoroughfares were blocked.

Of the more than four hundred people arrested yesterday evening, over two hundred were questioned over the night and re-leased. Many however will be indicted, it appears.

Some one hundred and fifty, mainly teenagers, still remain – chiefly because they refuse to identify themselves. They are thus continuing the extreme right wing program that began with the road blocking; attempting to show that massive arrests will shut down the police departments, the courts and the jails, and will make the Disengagement Plan (which they bitterly oppose) an impos-sible mission.

Last night the organizers issued a statement calling the event a "dizzying success." The National Home issued a statement say-ing: "Congratulations to all the Land of Israel loyalists who went with great dedication and blocked roads. The police preparations and all their attempts to stop us did not succeed. Today the people of Israel realize that the transfer affects every single person in the country. The police will not be able to prepare better than they did today. In the event that areas in the land of Israel are closed to Jewish travel, the whole country will be blocked. We call upon everyone to whom the land and the people of Israel are dear to their heart, to join us and join the struggle!"

The I.B.N. reporter paused a second. "Two of the leaders of the National Home were ordered released from prison today, after they were arrested two days ago. The court ordered them freed with restrictions, but their actual release has been held up to allow the prosecution to appeal the decision."

The reporter cleared her throat. "One kassam rocket fell to-day near..."

Miri turned the radio off. "You don't think Yair refused to identify himself, do you?" She asked, worried.

"No," Efrat replied quickly. "They wouldn't have let him call home if he hadn't identified himself."

"He might be on his way home already," Yoram said hopefully. "They might have questioned him last night and released him this morning!"

"But he would have called home!" Miri objected.

"Not if his cell phone needs recharging," Efrat mused out loud.

The front door opened. Yair stepped in.

"Yair!" They cried, and Miri ran to hug him.

"*Ima*, stop," he said embarrassed but pleased. "Look, I'm sorry I didn't call to say I was going with some friends to go block roads. I figured we'd only be gone for a few hours, and that I'd call as soon as we got back and I'd recharge my cell phone..."

Efrat looked smug.

"So what happened?" Yoram asked, looking ever so relieved.

Yair sat down at the table, and they all sat around him. "Well," he started, "We got there a bit early – at four thirty instead of five o'clock. There were some other people wearing Gush Katif shirts in the area. Well, we just walked around ignoring the nine police-men that were there... At five o'clock exactly, about ten protestors marched down the block and daringly sat in the middle of the gi-gantic intersection. My friends and I joined them and so did a lot of other people; soon the whole road was blocked in all directions. We tied our hands with orange tape so that the police and the me-dia would see that we didn't plan to use violence. Well, the police tried dragging us away. They kicked and cursed us (Miri stifled a gasp) but," Yair grinned, "we blocked that road for an hour! Many drivers eventually stopped beeping their horns and got out of their cars to join us. We sang and danced and handed them cold drinks and snacks. Apparently, they hadn't heard the news – either that or they didn't believe that we would manage to outsmart the police and actually block roads," Yair snickered.

"Eventually, police fired concussion grenades and a water cannon was brought to the scene as well, but a crowd ran towards it and blocked it some two hundred meters before it could reach the large intersection. Ten other guys and I were detained by the angry police and taken to the Russian Compound Prison. We were all in good spirits and said the evening prayers with the dozens of other protestors there.

After warning me not to participate in demonstrations for the next twenty four hours, they released me without restrictions," Yair sighed. "When I left, I saw dozens of parents whose children were still being detained in the compound, arguing with guards who wouldn't let them meet with their children or even bring them homemade food."

"Were all the policemen so nasty?" Efrat asked her brother.

"Look, I heard some guys saying that they were surprised to see that many of the police didn't exactly make the greatest efforts possible to drag them from the roads. However, I also heard one guy telling how he saw one policeman beating a boy, and the boy pleaded with him: "Stop hitting me, arrest me already! Just arrest me! Don't hurt me!" But the policeman didn't stop."

"Yair," Yoram said soberly to his son, "next time, call me! I won't prevent you from going, but I do want to be there with you."

A flash of happy surprise showed itself in Yair's tired face. "Thank you, *Aba!*" And after plugging in his cell phone to recharge it, Yair headed for a warm shower and a soft bed.

Chapter 26

Efrat was reading Avi Segel's article and laughing. Miri looked at her daughter, amazed. "My goodness, Effie, what's so funny? You've been laughing for the past ten minutes!"

Efrat wiped her streaming eyes. "Yes, because I keep rereading it. The article is actually rather sad since it's true, yet Avi Segel writes it in an extremely funny way:

From the Diary of the Minister for Interior Security

by Avi Segel (2005)
[Translated from the Hebrew by Shifra Shomron, BeSheva Newspaper, with permission]

Sunday, 19:00 – Tell Shimon Shifer that the extreme right is dangerous. That'll satisfy him for now.

Monday, 8:05 – Tell Rafi Reshef that the extreme right are planning something against the Prime Minister.

Monday, 10:30 – Ride on bus with journalists. If I don't have a different idea, I'll say that the next assassinator is already on his way.

Monday, 13:00 – Check if the conversation with Rafi appeared on the afternoon news.

Tuesday, all morning – A meeting with Tommy Lapid to agree on position. Agree with him that we shouldn't say exactly the same things about the extreme right.

Wednesday, 18:00 – Eureka, I've found it! The extreme right want to attack the Temple Mount. Develop the idea.

Wednesday, 19:00 – O.K. The extreme right wants to bomb the Temple Mount with planes. A bit absurd, but the media will buy it.

Wednesday, 21:30 – A conversation with the head of *Shabak* in order to verify positions. Agree with him not to say the exact same things about the extreme right.

Thursday, 7:00 – Last night I dreamt that once I was the extreme right. How strange.

Thursday, 16:00 – A press conference. Need something big... The extreme right are trying to drop a nuclear bomb on Jerusalem? To develop.

Friday, 12:00 – Hope the extreme right will start to really act, because I'm starting to run out of stories.

~ ~ ~

Efrat finished reading it to her mother, still laughing. Miri sighed. "I don't find it funny. It's too tragic!"

Efrat was still giggling, "Oh, but can't you see the funny side of it? The poor government minister; what ridiculous stories he's having to make up about us because we really aren't doing anything..."

Miri smiled at her daughter. "My dear, I've never known anyone to enjoy reading as much as you do. Why, I've seen you laughing while reading history books!"

Efrat nodded in agreement. "Well, yes. The history books I read are generally quite interesting and parts of them are funny. At least, to me."

"Oh, Effie. What are we going to do?" Miri sighed. "If Disengagement does happen..." her voice trailed off weakly.

Efrat put the newspaper down and looked at her mother, concerned. "What do your friends say? What does Mrs. Eisley say?" She asked.

"I can't talk to any of them about the possibility, however remote, of Disengagement occurring. In their opinion, even thinking that Disengagement might happen is a clear sign of lack of faith in G-d!"

"But, but how ridiculous!" Efrat sputtered. "I believe in G-d and so does *Aba*! And yet we both think that there's a likely chance that Disengagement will happen. How is it a lack of faith?"

"They think that it shows lack of faith," Miri answered calmly, "because they are convinced that it is such a horrible thing and that therefore G-d won't let it happen; it would be a desecration of His name. So, if you believe that Disengagement might happen, that means that you don't believe G-d will stop it, and that is lack of faith!"

"But why should G-d stop it? If we are stupid and sinful enough to dream up such a plan and seek to carry it out, then why shouldn't G-d punish us by letting such a plan happen?" Efrat was disgusted. "I don't agree at all with what they think! According to them, someone who thought before the Holocaust that a Holocaust might happen, would have been guilty of lack of faith!"

"Well," Miri sighed, "that is their mood, and I'm not trying to force them to change it. They are all hoping, praying and expecting that a big miracle will happen, that Disengagement won't happen and that we will all celebrate."

Efrat winced. "G-d help us!"

~~~

"*Aba*," Efrat said as she was walking that evening in the sand dunes with her father, Yair and Beauty. "*Aba*, what will happen to all those people who are so convinced a huge miracle will happen to prevent Disengagement? Will they have a huge crisis in their faith?"

Before Yoram could answer, Yair put in: "Hey, a huge miracle might still happen!"

"But you know the sages tell us that it is forbidden to rely on miracles," Efrat retorted quickly.

"True," Yair agreed. "And I'm not relying on miracles. I'm relying on the logical possibility that enough soldiers will refuse orders and enough people will block roads or come to the Gush to prevent Disengagement from happening."

"Well," Yoram said concerned, "you do realize that there is a possibility that Disengagement will happen?"

"Sure I realize that it can happen. I see how the army is preparing and how the media is egging it on. But I'm hopeful and I do see a possibility that it won't happen."

Yoram nodded. "As long as you realize that it can happen. I don't want you to be all shocked and broken up if it does happen," he said, patting Yair on the shoulder.

Yair smiled wanly. "*Aba*, if Disengagement does happen, we will all be shocked and broken up – even you who expect it to happen!"

Efrat nodded in agreement. "*Aba*, what will everyone do if we are kicked from our homes? Where will we go?"

A swift look of pain crossed Yoram's face. He pet Beauty's golden fur gently and thoughtfully. Finally he broke his silence. "Efrat, Yair," he started. "I'm the head of the family, and as head of the family I'm responsible for certain things – like making sure that there is a roof over our head and food on the table. Making sure that you two get an education, and that Yair can have the clarinet lessons he wants and so forth. It's a big responsibility as you'll find out when you're older and have children of your own. Well, contrary to what the community leaders are saying to their increased popularity, I don't want my family to end up in a tent or in a hotel for G-d knows how long; I'd have failed as head of the family."

"So have you decided where we'll live if we are expelled from the Gush?" Yair asked hesitantly. It was an awkward question for him to ask, and not one he would have dared ask if it hadn't been for the fact that they were way out in the sand dunes, surrounded only by the silent sand and rustling acacias.

You see, the Gush and every settler and many right wing people in the country were in the "home stretch" of the Anti Disengagement struggle. To accept that Disengagement was going to happen – and even to search for a place to live after Disengagement, was simply not done! It was paddling against the current of public Gush Katif opinion which was: IT isn't going to happen. We are preparing for the Redemption feast that will be in two months. And... if IT does happen, G-d forbid, then we'll go to tents and to hotels. We'll continue the struggle! We won't just disappear!

"I can't go to a hotel!" Yoram had exclaimed when he'd first heard this plan. "I've got three dogs! Where will I put them? I refuse to put them in the pound for months! And forget going to a tent; I'm not a teenager. I need a bed and a stove and a fridge and a bathroom and a shower... where will we do our laundry? I don't want to live in a tent for months. What will happen in winter?" And Miri had agreed with him.

Efrat repeated Yair's question: "So *Aba*, if the Gush is, G-d forbid, destroyed, where will we go to?"

"*Ima* and I will go next week and look at the Caravillas the government is putting down in Nitzan."

"Caravillas?" Efrat smirked. "What is that supposed to mean?"

"Haven't you heard of them?" Yair turned to his sister, surprised.

"Of course I've heard of them," Efrat answered defensively. "But I'm not sure what the word means, and I've never seen a picture of them."

"Caravilla," Yoram explained quietly, "is a mixture of the words 'caravan' and 'villa'. It is a good word because it describes the structures aptly; they are pre-fab houses, single story, three or four bedrooms. We'll tell you more about them once we've gone to see them."

Efrat hurried ahead uncomfortably. She hated such talk. Disengagement, worries, tents, struggles… she was sick of hearing about it. She bent down a bit and passed through an acacia tree. Its slender long green leaves were starting to turn a deep brown at the edges; the summer was hot and the leaves were drying up. Efrat continued walking, sometimes bending gracefully and passing through acacia trees – the dry leaves crackling beneath her sandals, and sometimes walking on the sand around the trees in her way. She could hear Yoram's and Yair's deep voices behind her as they followed more slowly.

Hearing heavy panting, Efrat stopped and turned around to see Beauty dashing up towards her.

"Oh Beauty, you darling!" Efrat exclaimed. She smiled sadly. "You don't have to worry about Disengagement, do you. Lucky you," she crooned and pet Beauty. Efrat sighed, "it's hard to be human, harder still to be a Jew, and even harder to be a Jew in Gush Katif in the month of Sivan 5765 (June 2005)."

Efrat sank down onto the still warm clean sand and waited for her father and brother to catch up. Beauty rested beside her, her red tongue hanging out.

The sky was pink towards the sea, light blue above Efrat's head and dark in the direction of Arab K'han Yunis. Efrat picked up a handful of sand and stared at it as she let the grains fall between her fingers and stream to the ground; the sand was composed of gold, light brown and dark brown grains as well as tiny white sea-shell fragments.

"Sand," she mused to herself. "Tiny grains of sand. So light and so small, any breeze can uproot them and cause them to fly distances away." She paused. "Yet these same grains prevent a mighty sea from flooding the country." She gazed at the darkening sky over K'han Yunis. "We too are grains of sand; small and weak – the government can move us, yet we prevent the Arabs from flooding the country with mortars and kassam rockets. When we are out of here and the army is out too, the Arabs will bring explosives in from Egypt without anyone to hinder them. From our Northern communities they'll be able to hit the city of Ashkelon and eventually Ashdod too." She picked up another handful of sand. "We are sand," she murmured, "no more and no less. Just sand."

Wednesday, 8 Sivan 5765 (June 15)

Dear Mem,

My Bible bagrut was today. My shield grade was one hundred – a bit higher than I thought I deserved. It was a long bagrut and it took me two hours and forty five minutes. Tiring. And I'm a bit worried that I didn't do very well.

Next week: bagruts in citizenship and then biology… Hashem help us!

Tomorrow evening is a formal farewell party for my grade; speeches, giving our teachers gifts… It will be on the lawn at the Ulpana. I expect it will be very touching.

Oh, Mem, I'm tired. And the nights are so hot that I don't manage to fall asleep until late and then I don't find my sleep refreshing. This makes me all the more tired.

Ima and Aba have decided we'll go to the Nitzan Caravilla site if we are expelled. That means we will have to work with SELA and get all our documents in order. I'm not happy about it, but we don't seem to have much of a choice.

Yesterday Yair and I made a birthday card for Aba. He is going to be fifty one!.

Good night,

Efrat.

Thursday, 9 Sivan (June 16), late at night

Dearest Mem,

I'm going to allow myself to ramble, so please be patient with me.

Just try to picture it, Mem: The lawn is long and wide, the grass is very green and lush, tall trees with maple like leaves are scattered in the grounds, huge Jerusalem stones compose a whitish man-made cliff, 130 white plastic chairs are arranged in a semi-circle on a small section of the lawn. A few tables with light refreshments; fruit, cakes, soft drinks… are attractively positioned. It is night time, and the moon shines brightly. Nary a cloud in the sky. Forty teenagers festively attired gather there together with their middle-aged parents.

Oh, Mem! It was lovely. The Rav's speech, the social director's speech, and a mother's speech – I wish I had their speeches taped! I nearly cried, in fact I would have if it weren't for the fact that my homeroom teacher was sitting beside me, and SHE was weeping. Sad as it was, there was also a pleasant blend of humor (yes!) and sweetness.

The speeches were about our being a light to others, creating a good atmosphere around us, keeping our eyes glued to the bright beacon of Torah light that will guide us no matter how black the darkness, to represent ourselves and the Gush truthfully and with honor, and… that we will always be warmly welcomed at the Ulpana ("so come back and visit!").

Then, after the speeches, we read short pieces about every teacher of ours (generally in rhymes) and handed each teacher a plant. Then the Ulpana called each girl by name to come receive her graduation certificate, a present (a book) and the grades picture etc. The names were not called by alphabetical order and I was a bit surprised when I suddenly heard my name being called. I quickly stepped forward and the Rav gave me my certificate and present etc. He also gave me a beaming yet gentle smile and a hearty wish of good luck! The principal gave her warm smile and shook my hand, and the two twelfth grade homeroom teachers insisted on a kiss and a handshake.

My grade gathered on the grass up front to sing our grade song (*sigh* four years at the Ulpana and our social director still hasn't managed to teach us to sing properly!).

Sad, so sad. And yet so very, very sweet. And because the sweetness and the sadness are both so poignant, salty tears are slowly running from the corners of my eyes and are gathering speed as they slide down my cheeks.

Oh, Mem! One field trip, one matconit, two more bagruts – and I'm done at the Ulpana. How have four years sped by so swiftly?!

And why does the shadow of Disengagement have to hover over everything?! Curse it!

Efrat.

Wednesday, 15 Sivan 5765 (June 22)

Dear Mem,

Finished reading all my citizenship material for the bagrut tomorrow. All that I have left is to go over my citizenship tests that I've done in the past year.

Mem, it was a lovely day! I managed to water my neighbor's garden, go on a walk in the dunes with Aba, Yair and Beauty, and read a book.

The sunset was absolutely gorgeous!

And right now I'm sitting on my bed, listening to the merry music from a wedding that is taking place in Neve Dekalim. So why am I suddenly so sad?

Mem, it could be the burden of being an adult, and it could be the numb feeling I get whenever I think of being uprooted from Neve Dekalim. Mem, I don't want to leave. Nobody does – and yet the I.D.F. will force us to go. And Mem, if our lives fall apart, then I want everything else to fall apart too. The entire country should come to a halt! Why should the country continue normally when Jews in Israel are being dragged from their homes?!

sigh Back on the dreaded subject again.

Mem, I want a vacation. I want to go somewhere where I can rest and relax – for a month at least. Somewhere where I won't hear discussion of Disengagement and where I'll be free from worrying about it. Perhaps on the moon?

Well, only citizenship and biology left. Thank Hashem, I only have two bagruts left! It's just too hard to concentrate on anything.

Efrat.

Thursday, 23 Sivan (June 30)

Dear Mem,

Yesterday my grade had a tour to the Holocaust Memorial Museum in Jerusalem, Yad VaShem. You can't finish twelve years of school in Israel and not be there at least once!

Mem, the new complex of the museum has done a wonderful job of blending the old with the modern; in every room were screens showing actual footage from those times, as well as screens showing survivors giving testimony, yet there were also diaries, pictures, Torah scrolls, cobble stones and train rails from the Warsaw ghetto (polished and clean but still very dreadful to walk on), shoes – dozens and dozens sunk in the floor under a protective piece of glass. There was also a room showing Nazi power. It shocked me. It was full of huge bright red Nazi flags, banners with black swastikas, screens showing Hitler giving speeches, and thousands and thousands of German soldiers marching…

I think that what moved me the most was the bluntness and simplicity of a fifteen year old who had written in his diary in English: "The Germans are sick!"

Mem, there is not the slightest need in the world to fly to Poland in order to learn about the Holocaust.

And after it all, one has to exit the museum and one finds oneself on an open plateau with the Jerusalem hills stretched out before you, a piney scent in the air and a hazy blue sky. It's hard.

On the way home from Jerusalem we saw policemen on every junction and corner – because the right wing organization called Beit Leumi planned to block roads again to protest the Disengagement Plan. Sadly the turn out was dismal. A pity.

Lots of mortars fell last night. Announcements to stay inside a protected area crackled. The phone repeatedly rang with Tzachi (Neve Dekalim phone network) recordings announcing mortars are falling and one must stay indoors. Yair and I weren't able to take Rufus and Beastie on a walk.

Well, I need to study for my biology bagrut.
Effie.

Friday, 24 Sivan (July 1)

Dear Mem,
We have lost a major, major battle! Right wing activists had recently moved into the abandoned hotel on the beach. Not everyone in the Gush got on with the outsiders, but there is no denying the fact that they came to help prevent Disengagement.

Anyhow, the government (or was it the courts?) decided that the hotel is an illegal outpost, and the soldiers closed the Gush for a day and evacuated the hotel! And we didn't even respond!!! In fact, a lot of youth are pleased that those people are out of the Gush – as I said, many didn't get along with them.

Are we stupid?! The Gush Katif hotel was evacuated and all us Gush Katif residents did to stop it – was precisely NOTHING! It's a filthy black stain on Gush Katif's conscience.

Efrat.

Chapter 27

Tamuz (July). The very hot summer month of Tamuz. And in the year 5765, Tamuz was extraordinarily hot in more ways than one.

But right now it was cool for it was still early morning. Efrat and Yair had taken the two smaller dogs Beastie and Rufus for a walk as soon as Yair had returned from *Shul*.

"Summer Vacation," Efrat commented to her brother. "I've always loved summer vacation! Yet somehow this summer vacation isn't fun at all."

Yair agreed. "I'd almost rather be learning. You know, Effie, I've hardly learned at all this entire year. We've hardly learned half as much as we should have, and that'll boomerang back at us next year – no matter what happens this summer."

Efrat smiled smugly, "Well, I've finished all my bagruts."

"Lucky you," Yair said enviously.

"So what are you planning to do now that the bagruts are over for this year, and summer vacation has really begun?" Efrat asked curiously.

Yair yanked Rufus to stop his pulling and answered, "I'll continue struggling against Disengagement. We're planning a lot of activities for this month. We only have about a month left until the government starts trying to implement their crazy scheme. And these activities ought to have a large turnout because all the youth are off from school now."

"Sure," Efrat said. "And we can all demonstrate peacefully, hand out thousands of orange ribbons and 'paint the country orange'. How nice!" Efrat retorted sarcastically.

Yair grimaced. "Stop it, Effie."

"I'm sorry," she apologized. "It's just that I've lost faith in preventing our expulsion."

"Don't say that too loudly," Yair cautioned her. "You'll be rather unpopular around here if you do."

Efrat just shrugged. "Yair, for all your activities against Disengagement, you still haven't been brainwashed into believing that a huge miracle is about to happen; and a huge Redemption feast is right around the corner. You are still a logical person. Tell me honestly, do you really believe that we can prevent Disengagement?"

Yair answered gravely and uncharacteristically, choosing his words carefully: "Prevent it? Yes, we have the power to prevent it. The problem is that the majority of our public will never take the drastic steps needed to prevent it. We know that Disengagement is terrible, but we don't really know quite how terrible it really is. And Disengagement is just an introduction to worse things, you know. If we really wanted to do everything possible to prevent it, then every settler and right wing person in this country would quit their job and camp-out in Gush Katif for a month. The elderly and those who couldn't come would instead block roads every day. We would incite the Arabs and that would keep the soldiers elsewhere fighting the real enemy. All soldiers who are religious or right wing would publicly refuse orders and come join us. All the Rabbis would encourage refusing orders; so far only ninety something year old former chief Rabbi and head of Mirkaz HaRav Yeshiva, the *Rav* Shapira, has publicly said according to the Torah and Jewish law one must refuse orders. Unfortunately, several Rabbis have said publicly to obey orders, and most of the Rabbis refuse to give a clear answer. This is a huge mistake – the Rabbinical Leadership should be clear."

Efrat said as Yair paused, "You've just said that the majority of the public won't take the steps needed to prevent Disengagement, so why are we bothering with futile demonstrations? It's just a huge waste of time and money."

"That bothered me too, Effie, until I read what a *Rav* wrote on the subject in the BeSheva newspaper."

"What did he say?"

"He said that according to the Sages, one has an obligation to protest in order to try and prevent the sin and in order to show the severity of the sin." Yair chuckled.

"What is so funny?"

"I'm just thinking, you are sick of discussing Disengagement and so am I, and yet we keep coming back to this distasteful subject – even when we do try and talk of something else!"

Efrat's pretty face tightened in determination. "You are right, Yair. Come, let us prove to ourselves that it is still possible to take a long walk and not mention Disengagement!"

Yair looked down at Effie, and for a few seconds their eyes twinkled. "Fine," he said. "Pick a topic to talk about."

"Um," Efrat struggled to find a subject. "We can't talk about summer vacation, can't wonder about next year…"

"Can't talk about politics, or the security situation," Yair put in cheerfully. "Can't gossip about neighbors or friends either," he added grinning.

Efrat glared at her brother. "Fine, then you think of something!"

"No problem," he assured her. Silence ensued for some minutes until Yair declared brightly: "We'll talk of music!"

Efrat laughed. "You mean you'll talk and I'll listen."

"Fair enough," Yair agreed. "My clarinet teacher wants to start teaching me to play jazz. He thinks that now that I know how to play klezmer and classical music, I should start learning…"

That walk, Yair and Efrat discussed music, books and finally the weather. It was a walk they would both remember for many, many years to come; struggling to find topics not immediately connected to Disengagement, and preventing the conversation from twisting to Disengagement related talk. It wasn't an easy task at all.

For instance, when they were discussing music, Yair had to remember not to discuss the new disc of anti-Disengagement songs that had recently come out. When they discussed books, Efrat had to remember not to discuss historical events she had read about that might have a bearing on Disengagement (like former Prime Minister Menachem Begin giving away the Sinai and evacuating the Jewish settlements there). Only the weather was a completely safe topic, since neither of them felt inclined to say "if there are sand storms, it might hinder the soldiers." Yes, the weather was a safe topic, but it was also a very boring one, and they had soon said all that could be said, and they walked the rest of the way home in silence.

Back home, Efrat pondered the conversation she and Yair had just had. "Why was it so hard for us to think about what to talk about? After all, we always found plenty to talk about before the Disengagement Plan, so why was it so hard now?" She ran her slender fingers through her wavy brown hair. "Oh, come on, Effie," she scolded herself. "You know very well that Disengagement has become such a major part of your life that small wonder you had a hard time finding something else to talk about!"

Efrat walked over to her mantelpiece and straightened the bric-a-brac absentmindedly. "I wonder what anti-Disengagement activities they have planned," she said softly. "I wonder."

But even the gloomy darkness of Disengagement closing in around them, couldn't quite stifle the natural summer joy. They went to the beach and also took many walks in the sand dunes. They took Beauty and Rufus to the manmade reservoir between Gadid and Gan-Or –

but soon the water there had all dried up in the summer heat, leaving only the thick black plastic lining showing.

One evening the Yefets had invited the Eisleys over. They were all sitting outside on plastic chairs underneath the grapevines since it was cooler outside than in the house.

Mrs. Eisley suddenly dropped a bombshell by saying: "Tomorrow our guests arrive. They are good friends of ours; we've known them for years.

They, their three sons, and two daughters will be smuggling in to the Gush tomorrow morning and will be staying with us until, well, until whenever. Until the Redemption feast."

Efrat stared at Mr. Eisley. He didn't look very pleased over his wife's announcement but he did look determined.

"Yes," Mrs. Eisley continued proudly. "We are doing our part. The Anti Disengagement Committee asked everyone to invite more people and get them into the Gush as soon as possible, and that is precisely what we are doing." Mrs. Eisley puffed herself up. "It will, of course, be very uncomfortable; all the laundry and more food to cook, not to mention the lack of privacy and the need to entertain our guests. But no one said it would be easy to stop Disengagement."

Perhaps Mrs. Eisley had seen the look on her husband's face, because she hurriedly changed the subject. "Tonight there is going to be another public burning of letters we got from SELA."

"What a shame," Yoram said. "I'm rather curious to read mine."

"Nah," Mrs. Eisley waved a hand in dismissal. "It's just a bunch of bunk."

"Well," Yoram said firmly, "I would have liked to have seen that for myself. I don't like my mail being destroyed before I've even had a chance to read it."

"But that is the whole point," Mrs. Eisley chuckled. "We want to show SELA that their letter is so extremely unimportant to us that we are burning it without even having opened it!"

Yoram shrugged. "Come, it's time to go to the synagogue."

The men left and Mrs. Eisley returned home to prepare for her guests. Efrat and Miri stayed sitting under the grapes.

"I don't like it, *Ima*. All these strange people pouring into the Gush. Some of them are fine people here to help us prevent Disengagement, but not all of them are like that. Why, some aren't even religious; what are they doing in our religious community? They should go the secular communities in the Gush!"

Miri sighed. "True. For years Neve Dekalim has had an acceptance committee; not just anyone could move here – you had to be religious. Now, whoever manages to slip past the soldiers is in and there's nothing we can do about it."

Yoram and Yair returned home very disgruntled.

"Synagogue was completely full. So many outsiders here now, that there aren't enough seats for everyone," Yair explained.

"We're going to have to get to the synagogue early on *Shabbat* or someone else will have taken our seats," Yoram warned.

But it was only after Efrat went on a walk that night with Yair, Rufus and Beastie, that she really understood. "My goodness! We have walked all around Neve Dekalim and we have only seen strangers. I wouldn't have thought that possible!"

Yair had a strange expression on his face. "You know, I wish I had some way of letting all these outsiders know that I'm not an outsider. That I really live here."

"Where are they all sleeping?" Efrat wondered.

"A lot are at families, and others are at the schools sleeping in the classrooms. It's really amazing to see their dedication for the cause!"

Efrat nodded. "I don't really like it. I mean, I know it is necessary and that the more people who come here the better, but, well, don't you feel that the Gush is turning into a demonstration? Right now, I feel like Neve Dekalim has turned into Zion Square!"

Yair just grinned. "You'll get used to it."

Efrat didn't grin back. "Do you think that they will get used to mortars and kassam rockets?"

Yair shrugged. "If they are here long enough, then yes, they will."

"Do you think *Ima* and *Aba* will invite some of the outsiders to stay with us?"

"I hope not; Beastie would go nuts, not to mention the rest of us…"

"How on earth are the Eisleys and all the others putting up with it?"

Yair chuckled. "You heard Mrs. Eisley – it is all part of our glorious struggle against Disengagement."

"Mr. Eisley didn't seem quite as enthusiastic about this part of 'the glorious struggle'," Efrat commented.

Yair nodded. "Mr. Eisley is so convinced that Disengagement will not happen that he doesn't think we need struggle so hard. Besides, he is a very private person and I'm sure that he is not pleased about having other people constantly in his house, even if they are old friends."

Efrat suddenly caught Yair by his shirt sleeve. "Yair! Look!"

"What?"

"Over there, in that garden. See – the 8-10 meter long red ocean freight container under the tree!"

"Oh!"

"What is it?"

"Exactly what you think it is," Yair replied knowingly. "It's a moving container, for that family to store all their possessions in."

Efrat was shocked. "So they have completely given up; they are leaving!"

"Yes," Yair said solemnly. "I'm afraid, Effie, that this sight is going to become more and more common the closer we get to the expulsion date."

"It is not a very nice sight."

"No, Effie. It is not. It's the sight of Neve Dekalim falling apart."

"I bet the Eisleys will be furious at them. Mrs. Eisley for sure will be very angry."

"Maybe."

"Well, if the Eisleys are mad at them then it is only to their own shame – not to that family's."

"Why do you say that?"

Efrat explained: "Even though it is summer vacation, we keep having gatherings at the *Ulpana* – you know, to talk things over. And at the last gathering, the *Rav* warned us that people that we know were going to start packing and leaving. And he told us that he doesn't blame them or judge them the less for the decisions they make. He told us that he salutes anyone who lived here in the Gush for the past five years under mortars and kassam rockets, and who has lasted this long in spite of the government and the media."

"The *Rav* said all that?"

"Yes."

"So he thinks Disengagement will happen?"

"Not necessarily, but he thinks it possible that it will."

"So why isn't he packing?"

"We actually did ask him that. And he said that he hopes

Disengagement doesn't happen, and that if it does, well, things are going to be a mess regardless and they might as well be a bit more of a mess."

Yair chuckled.

"Hey, Yair, look – there's another container!"

~~~

"Yair!" Miri called. "Are you coming with us to the Eisleys to meet their guests?"

Yair shrugged. "Do I have to?"

"Well, they do have three boys around your age. You could show them around."

"No, I'm not showing three strangers around; I'm not a tour guide. I'm going to go talk to the soldiers at Kissufim," Yair said stubbornly.

"Didn't Yair seem a bit bitter?" Miri asked her daughter as Yair stomped away.

"*Ima*, this is a tough time for Yair. Expect him to be a bit bitter."

"What about you, Efrat? Are you going to come with me to welcome the Eisley's guests?"

"Um, no. I've got a book to read." And Efrat disappeared into the safety of her room.

That night, the atmosphere was a bit strained at the Yefet dinner table. Yoram, Efrat and Yair were silent and only Miri gushed about how very nice the Eisley's guests were.

Yair finally lost his patience. "*Ima*, I don't care how nice they are! They are outsiders, strangers. What do they know about what we are going through? They aren't the ones about to be kicked from their homes!"

"Yes," Efrat chimed in. "They come here a month before the expulsion date and think that they are helping. They are just tourists! They come here for the beach and the dunes and the excitement. And when it is all over they have their house to return to."

"Wait a second," Miri said, surprised. "We, the Gush, have been asking people to come here. We've been advertising and practically begging for people to come. And now people finally are coming and you two are resentful?"

"Yeah, I'm resentful! Now, a month before Disengagement when it is summer vacation and the kids are bored they suddenly all remember to come. Come to Gush Katif – the exciting summer camp! Where were they half a year ago when Sharon was still planning Disengagement?!" Yair stormed out of the kitchen.

Miri half rose to go after him.

"Leave him alone," Yoram advised her. "He'll calm down soon enough; he just needs to let off some steam."

And sure enough, an hour later Yair came quietly back into the house and straight to his room. Five seconds later and the pure sounds of the clarinet were heard at full blast.

But little run-ins with the outsiders were constantly occurring.

"Yair and I had to get some outsiders out of our chairs in the synagogue. I mean, really, we paid for those seats! Why didn't they sit on plastic chairs instead of taking other peoples' chairs?" Yoram complained that *Shabbat* evening.

And when they took Beauty and Rufus out to run in the sand dunes after the *Shabbat* morning meal:

"Oh, no!" Efrat exclaimed. "People ahead."

And when Efrat went to the library on Sunday she found it packed with dozens of people she had never seen before. All the computers, sofas and arm chairs were taken, and many of the outsiders were loudly talking on their cell-phones.

Efrat turned to find a good book and couldn't help hearing snatches of:

"...so we got in the car, but we didn't know the way, and we must've taken a wrong turn... suddenly all these Arab houses..."

Efrat sighed and walked to a different section in the library.

"...and buy two milks and a loaf of bread. What? Oh, I'm staying at Shirat HaYam..."

Efrat quickly checked a book out and left the library. "I'm not going there again for a while," she muttered to herself. And she walked home swiftly, ignoring all the obnoxious reporters and well meaning outsiders.

"Efrat, have you heard?" Yair asked her as soon as she opened the front door.

"No, what?"

"The new big anti Disengagement activity is reaching K'far Maimon and marching from there to Gush Katif! The Rabbis are calling on everyone to make it, and the Yesha Council is promising that nothing will stop them from marching en masse to the Gush!"

"Wow," Efrat paused. "If they all really do march to the Gush, we might prevent Disengagement after all!"

"Well, we will find out soon enough. It is supposed to take place on Monday the 11th of Tamuz (July 18th)."

"Oh, Yair! If only..."

"Yes. If only."

And then there was nothing more to be said.

The BeSheva newspaper started advertising full page ads calling on everyone to come to K'far Maimon.

An *advertisement for the Giant March to Gush Katif, BeSheva newspaper*

More and more outsiders reached the Gush. Unknown youth walking around the community and hanging out at the pizza parlor and all the unknown adults setting up new blogs at the library on their laptops had become a common sight. The Eisley's guests gave a nightly Torah lesson that Miri attended regularly to please Mrs. Eisley.

Efrat was amused to see Yair giving directions to the zoo to a bunch of outsiders:

"Just turn your car around 180 degrees and drive straight," Yair said speaking slowly, with a shocked look on his handsome face. "It's opposite the gas station; you can't miss it!"

The driver thanked Yair and sped off.

Efrat laughed. "Why so shocked, Yair? How should an outsider know where the zoo is?"

"This is Neve Dekalim, not Tel-Aviv. How could he NOT know where the zoo is?!" Yair retorted irritably.

"Hey, Yair. If K'far Maimon works, there could be tens of thousands of outsiders here."

"G-d bless them."

Soldiers and settlers during prayer time in K'far Maimon...,
BeSheva 2005

But Neve Dekalim wasn't to see its gates flooded with people sailing through to stop Disengagement. The 15,000 people never got past K'far Maimon. The police set up a fence around K'far Maimon and threatened to use live fire on anyone trying to break out from K'far Maimon towards Gush Katif. The police stopped buses from driving down south to K'far Maimon by confiscating the bus drivers' licenses. The people who had managed to gather at K'far Maimon remained there for three days before giving up and dispersing.

There had been a group who wanted to storm through the fence and reach Gush Katif, but the Rabbis and the other people in charge there prevented them from doing so.

And yet the Rabbis and settler leaders tried to brand K'far Maimon as a success! All except for one Knesset Member who was disgusted by the K'far Maimon episode, and called on everyone to try and reach Gush Katif by any means they could.

Efrat was feeling very sad towards the end of the month of Tamuz. One morning she saw a letter lying on her desk. It was from the *Ulpana*. Curious, she opened it. It was from the *Rav*, a letter written by him to her grade in order to strengthen and encourage them. Efrat read it and wept.

A few hours later she listened to the news. A few more soldiers had refused orders and had been sentenced to 28 days in jail. Leaves falling in a forest, Efrat sighed and walked outside. Sunset. The sky over the sea was a flooded dull orange. The sky was hazy. In fact, the sea, the palm trees, the dunes – all seemed somewhat faded like they were slipping away and leaving her.

"No!" Efrat said hotly. "No, it's not fair. If I have to go through Disengagement, then so do you. You can't just slip away and leave us here to deal with the mess! You can't! Can't!"

"What is the matter?" Yair asked her when he saw her sitting under a tree, facing the sea and sobbing.

"Yair, it's all hazy...leaving...the spirit of the Gush...leaving...slipping away..."

"Effie," her brother said softly. "Not to upset you, but Gush Katif HAS left us. We are not in Gush Katif anymore. We are just in a poster of Gush Katif. A picture. And it is hazy because the colors are all running together and dripping off the poster." He smiled grimly.

"Gush Katif herself is beyond the army's reach. This – this is just a poster."

Efrat smiled between her tears. "But we have pictures and memories of the real thing."

"They can never take that away from us," Yair assured her.

Chapter 28

2 Av (August 7, 2005)

"Where are the children?" Miri asked Yoram.

"They said something about going out to the sand dunes to collect some sand," Yoram said from behind the day's newspaper.

"What on earth does that mean? Why collect sand?" Miri asked trying to make sense out of her husband's words.

"I would think it obvious," Yoram muttered.

Miri suddenly gasped. "Oh my G-d, the poor dears! I see it now. They want to collect sand as a last memoir, as a souvenir from Neve Dekalim." Tears filled her eyes. "Oh, Yoram, we should go too. We can't let them do it by themselves!"

Yoram neatly folded the newspaper and placed it on the kitchen table. "I'll just get my hat and sunglasses."

Mr. and Mrs. Yefet walked to the end of the street and then out into the sand dunes. They walked together in silence for a while; the sea breeze refreshingly cool on their faces, the sun rays beating down from above and the heat rising shimmering from beneath their feet.

"Yoram, they could be anywhere out here."

"They might be, but I rather think I know where they are. They are most likely to be on top of *Kir HaMavet*, the wall of death. It isn't much further."

Kir HaMavet was a name that had stuck to a large sand dune because of the rumor that an off-road vehicle had crashed down it killing the passenger. This name was peculiarly apt to describe the last place that Efrat and Yair felt compelled to go.

"Why would they go there?" Miri asked, not understanding.

But all Yoram would say in reply was: "Nice view from there."

They reached Kir HaMavet and climbed up it. It wasn't easy

climbing up such a steep sand dune. They found Efrat and Yair sitting on top, slowly filling a bottle with clean golden sand. They both stopped and looked sadly up as Miri and Yoram sank down on the sand next to them.

"I've seen pictures," Efrat said softly, "of Gush Katif before we settled it. It was all wild sand dunes before we came, and it'll go back to being wild sand dunes after we leave."

"Right," Yair agreed. "Because the army will smash up all our homes, the sand will drift and cover up all the rubble again."

Yoram put a hand on his son's shoulder. "You two will rebuild it one day. I don't know how many years it will take, but one year..." His voice trailed off as he gazed intently at the horizon.

Miri spoke brightly, "Of course you'll come back, we all will! Come on, let's finish filling this bottle."

Efrat and Yair gave their mother an amused look, and continued filling the bottle.

"Two more weeks," Yair mused, screwing the cap onto the bottle. "Two more weeks, maybe less, and the soldiers will be here."

"Two more weeks, that doesn't give us much time," Efrat answered.

"Much time for what?" Yoram wanted to know.

"Much time to say farewell to the Gush," Efrat replied. "But then, perhaps we shouldn't say farewell."

"Yeah, farewell is so final," Yair responded. "*Ima, Aba,* what are we going to do when the soldiers come?" Yair asked troubled.

"I don't know," Miri answered, struggling to keep her voice steady and cheerful. "I suppose we could have them help us pack."

"Yes, I suppose," Efrat said doubtfully.

The four of them sat on the sand, high up on a sand dune facing the sea. To their left were Gadid hothouses, to their right were the white houses and-red tiled roofs of Neve Dekalim and far behind them was gray forbidding Arab K'han Yunis.

"Quite a few people have bought ocean freight containers or hired moving trucks, perhaps we ought to also," Yoram wondered out loud.

"Did you see that interview with Mrs. Eisley?" Yair grinned. "She was loudly insisting to the reporter that she wasn't going to pack, but her house was half empty!"

"It isn't funny, Yair," Miri admonished.

"Well, I wish people would at least be honest," Yair retorted.

Slowly the Yefet family got to their feet. They turned away from gazing at the sea and walked back home. Yair clutched the precious bottle of sand tightly.

Sunday, 2 Av 5765 (August 7)

Dear Mem,

All the regional council workers and the mayor of Gush Katif have been fired by the government.

There is very little food left in the grocery store; rumor has it that they aren't ordering more food.

Monday, 3 Av 5765 (August 8)

Dear Mem,

A lot of different moving trucks can be seen around Neve Dekalim. Some of the trucks are actually orange!

I hardly see anyone I know anymore – so many outsiders. Still, in a way it makes things easier.

Monday, 10 Av 5765 (August 15)

Dear Mem,

The fast day yesterday was horrid. In the synagogue, we were all sitting and mourning for the destruction of The Temple. As we read the scroll of Eicha mourning the fall of Jerusalem, we felt that every word applied to the Gush! Oh, my Gush! My lovely, lovely home. I've lost you forever! And yet the preparations for the Redemption feast go on… Oh, if only!

Wednesday, 12 Av 5765 (August 17)

Dear Mem,

All I have are four words to write to you and then I'll put you in a box too, and not reopen you until, well, until – I'm not sure when. I think the government is sending us all on buses to different hotels, but we will go to our Nitzan Caravilla.

Anyhow, the four words are: The soldiers are here!

Oh, and Mem, sorry but I see I have to add this: Ima is crying. Two soldiers are carrying Yair who is struggling. Aba has the dogs. Some plovers are trilling overhead very loudly. And now the soldiers are coming for me! So in you go, into the big brown box.

Bye Mem,
Effie.

A dream of 30 years...

...destroyed in a few moments

Oh grains and grains of golden sand
What is to be my fate?
I have lost you from my land
I have lost you from my state!

Photographs on the previous page were made by Eran Sterenberg. Adapted from a pamphlet of Gush Katif Public Relations, courtesy of Dror Vanunu.

Glossary

Aba - Hebrew for father

Bagrut - Israel matriculation exam
Bar Mitzvah - the thirteenth birthday marking a Jewish boy's acceptance of the commandments
Beit Midrash - a religious study hall
Brit Mila - ritual circumcision

Chanukiah - candelabrum used on Jewish festival of Chanukah

Davening - praying

Gemara - Talmud
Gush Katif - Block of Jewish communities in the Gaza Strip

Hagomel - blessing recited when saved from harm
Hallel - a special prayer said on holidays
Hamotzei - blessing over bread
Hamsin - a heat wave
Haredi - ultra-Orthodox
Hashem - a Hebrew name of G-d
Hashmonian - Maccabees and their ruling descendents

Intifada - name of Arab uprising/war
Ima - Hebrew for mother

Judenrein - free of Jews (German)

Klezmer - Jewish jazz music
Kiddush - blessing recited over wine on the Sabbath
Kippa - Hebrew for skullcap

Lecha Dodi - song to welcome, usher in the Sabbath

Machon HaMikdash - the Temple Institute
Matnas - community center
Matconit - internal school exam given before the matriculation exam
Midrachov - pedestrian mall
Mikva - ritual bath
Minyan - quorum of 10 men for prayer
Moshav(im) - agricultural cooperative community

Olim - Jews who immigrate to Israel

Rav - Hebrew for Rabbi
Rotem - a type of desert flower

Sabra - Jews born in Israel
SELA - Agency to assist Gush Katif and N. Shomron evacuees
Shabak - internal Israel security service
Shabbat - Hebrew for Sabbath
Shalom Aleichem - Sabbath song sung upon returning home from synagogue
Shamash - the candle used for lighting the other candles in a chanukiah
Shiur - lesson
Shul - synagogue
Siddur(im) - prayer book(s)
Slichot - special prayers said before Jewish New Year
Succah - temporary dwelling during Succot
Succot - Feast of Tabernacles

Tanach - bible
Tashlich - Service to symbolically cast away one's sins at the New Year
Tshuva - repentance

Ulpana - religious girls' high school

Yashar Koach - words of praise for a deed well done
Yeshiva - religious boys' high school

Zmironim - song books

An Interview
With Shifra Shomron

Website: *www.geocities.com/nevedekalim*
Email: *nevedekalim@yahoo.com*

What motivated you to write Grains Of Sand: The Fall Of Neve Dekalim?
I felt an urge to set down on paper, blue ink on white pages, what I was experiencing and what I saw going on around me. I can't quite explain it – even to myself. I felt a great urge to write and once I started to obey it the pen moved as if on its own accord. Writing gave me a sense of satisfaction of inner peace.

What do you hope to accomplish by telling this story?
I hope that my book will enable people to understand what we, the people of Gush Katif, went through. I hope to put a human face on what have been just facts, numbers. And I hope that the person reading my book will, for a few hours, be transferred beyond time and beyond location – into my Gush Katif.

How did you decide on the characters in your book?
I knew I wanted my characters to express and represent many of the different thoughts and emotions the people of Gush Katif had. On the other hand, I didn't want too many characters because it gets difficult to keep track of them and becomes confusing for the author and the reader. I settled on four main characters – all of whom have strong personalities and share their thoughts and feelings.

How long did it take you to write this book?
The first draft took me a year to write. I started the book in the month of Nissan 5765 (April 2005) while I was still a twelfth grader. Once the book was written, it took me an additional month to type it up.

You were a senior in the Neve Dekalim religious girls' high school when you wrote this book. Was it hard to write a book, and concentrate on your studies, with mortars and rockets targeting your community?

Curiously enough, it wasn't very difficult. I concentrated on my studies as a way of escaping the difficult situation of living under the shadows of Arab terror and Disengagement. Writing my book took on a form of therapy. However, most of the book was written after the unforgivable Disengagement. I started planning the book and wrote the first chapters as a senior, but the book was accomplished the following year when I was doing National Service.

Did you also attend demonstrations?

Yes, I did. How could I not? I didn't attend every single demonstration though – for instance if I had an important test the following day.

You must be very disciplined. Were you a good student?

Yes, I was a very good student. Following my high school graduation I received a "Letter of Excellence" from the Ministry of Education.

Do you think people might dismiss your writing because of your age?

They might. I should hope though that they would give me a chance and at least open the book. Let me add that many people who have read my articles have been very surprised to discover that I was a teenager.

You mention writing articles. Could you elaborate?

During the past few years I have written and published numerous articles and several poems. I've also translated some articles and poems.

You were raised in Israel yet you wrote this book in English. Why did you choose to write it in English and not Hebrew?

I was raised in Israel yet English is my mother tongue. Also, there is a far larger English readership for the book than a Hebrew readership and I am interested in as many people as possible reading my book.

Who did you first tell you were writing this book and why?

I first told my mother. She taught me to read when I was four years old and has been my English teacher throughout my elementary and high-school years.

Was it hard to find a publisher for your book?

Both yes and no. While looking for a publisher I came in email contact with an author who has worked with Chaim Mazo and praised him highly. I'm very pleased and excited to be with Mazo publishers. Otherwise, there were several publishers interested in reading my manuscript yet weren't interested in publishing it. I received some impersonal form letter rejections and also some very encouraging ones. For example, one publisher's rejection letter gave me a list of possible people with contact information who might be able to help me in publishing my book.

Would you like to see your book made into a movie?

It depends. My book deals with a very sensitive subject and I don't think it is easily portrayed.

Besides writing, how do you spend your free time?

I love taking walks in nature with my family and our pet dogs. I also enjoy painting, reading a good book, and listening to Celtic music.

What makes a good book for you?

A good book for me is a book which tells a good story realistically and is well written.

Who are your favorite authors and why?

P.G. Wodehouse because his books really make me laugh and J.R.R. Tolkien because I've yet to read a fantasy book more realistically and richly told.